At the master's hand sat a woman with ink-black hair piled high, glittering dark eyes in an ivory face with a knife-sharp profile. *How beautiful she is!* Daphne thought quickly. And then: *like a wild animal. A leopard, with white teeth and sharp claws.*

The woman's black eyes met Daphne's. A chill went through the girl as she moved toward the table, where a fourth place was set and waiting. The woman's gaze was like a magnet.

She's beautiful, Daphne thought again, sinking into the chair the old servant was holding for her.

Beautiful and evil, and she hates me already. Why?

THE SECRET OF THE BAYOU

by

FRANCINE DAVENPORT

ace books
A Division of Charter Communications Inc.
1120 Avenue of the Americas
New York, N.Y. 10036

An Ace Book

I

"We'll be comin' into Fairlawn Station in a few minutes now, ma'am."

Daphne Summerfield turned away from the dust-streaked train window and smiled into the conductor's serious face. "I didn't know there was a town. I was under the impression from Mr. Osborne's letter—"

"That's right, miss. It's right out in the country. Nothin' there but the deepo and a little general store." His speech was slurred so that she had to listen carefully. "Station's named for Fairlawn Plantation, though. Ever'thing in this part of the country used to belong to the Osbornes. You'll be right glad to arrive, I reckon."

Daphne's answering smile was uncertain. She wasn't going to admit it to a stranger, but for the last hour, as the train slipped through the oddly foreign-looking countryside, she had been quivering with nervous anticipation of the unknown future. *Why did I ever set off on this wild-goose chase?* she asked herself miserably, feeling much younger than her twenty years.

It had seemed reasonable as well as adventurous when Mary Lee Brewster, the minister's young wife, suggested that she take a post as governess in faraway Louisiana. "After all, Daphne honey, I came here to Maine from Virginia, and they're as different as day and night. Not but

5

what I've been right happy here, even if the snow is chin-deep from November to April. I reckon I'd be happy anywhere with Loren."

"You have a husband to look after you," Daphne reminded her. "I'll be alone in the world."

Mary Lee smiled. "Who knows? You may find yourself a husband in Fairlawn, Louisana!"

"Right now I'm more interested in earning a living," Daphne retorted with some spirit. "I certainly don't want to stay here now that Granny's gone and Uncle John's family will be moving into her house." Her voice wavered, but she set her soft little chin. "After all, I've taught the village school three winters now. I'll soon be a dried-up old maid like Miss Prudence Willis."

Mary Lee patted her shoulder. "Then I'll just write to Cousin Charles Osborne and tell him you'll be glad to look after his little girl," she said softly. "After all, his mother and mine were girlhood friends in the Tidewater, and even though we've never met I just know you'll like Cousin Charles. All the men in that family are good-lookin' and have beautiful manners."

"But he's married," Daphne felt obliged to remind her.

"To a Spanish lady, too. It's purely romantic."

Daphne said primly, "I don't expect to find anything romantic about another woman's husband."

Now, three weeks later, she shivered a little in spite of the thick damp heat that pressed down upon her. The little white frame house where she had lived with Granny since the death of her parents seemed very dear and far away, the village school a safe refuge. What was she doing in this place where the very earth was a strange red color and the grass looked like knife blades instead of being softly green? Even the trees were unfamiliar, and webs of a misty gray substance hung from their branches.

"Is there anything I can do for you before we get there, ma'am?"

"No, thank you."

You can't turn back now, Daphne Summerfield, she admonished herself sternly. She smoothed her gored blue serge skirt and settled the black silk tie that set off her plain white shirtwaist. Little golden-brown tendrils had escaped from under the brim of her straw sailor; she tucked them back in place, using the blurry windowpane as a mirror. She was glad that Granny hadn't wanted her to wear mourning—there was mighty little money for new clothes, anyway—but even in this stern schoolmarm garb she looked younger than her twenty years. The face that looked back at her from the train window had big violet-blue eyes set about with dark lashes and a delicately chiseled pink mouth with a dimple at each side. She wished that she looked just a little older. Not like Miss Prudence Willis, who had been doing plain sewing for folks since before she, Daphne, was born, but a little more like a governess. People expected her to look prim and stern. Meeting her for the first time, no one would ever guess what good order she could keep in a schoolroom full of lively big boys, or how well her pupils took to learning.

The train slowed to a stop. The conductor brought her valise down from the rack and said kindly, "Just follow me, ma'am. Looks like you're expected, all right. That's Mistah Miguel over by the store, with the rig from Fairlawn."

A little old man with a brown nutcracker face hobbled across the yard of the combined depot and crossroads store. Seeing Daphne descending the train steps, he bobbed a quaint bow. *"Buenas dias, señorita.* The buggy, she's here. Me, I'm Miguel." He took her valise from her—it was almost as big as he was—and limped toward the light buggy.

Daphne followed, trying to control her shaking knees. She asked in a subdued voice, "How did you know me?"

Miguel gave her a friendly grin as he unwrapped the reins from the whip-socket. "Nobody else for here, not for a long time," he explained with a cackling laugh. "This ees far from everywhere, *señorita.* That is one reason my master wants a friend for Isabella."

Once more Daphne felt the strange chill that had swept over her on the train. What was in store for her in this strange, hot country? To take her mind off her fears as she settled down beside Miguel, she asked, "What is the strange stuff on the trees? It looks like—like ghost hair."

"Spanish moss, *señorita.* Have you ever seen a ghost, that you know what his hair looks like?"

Daphne tried to laugh. "I don't believe there is such a thing. Do you?"

"I don't know. Witches, *si,* I believe in witches, all right." Miguel crossed himself hastily. "They are very powerful. In Spain we know these things." He gave her a sidelong look. She shivered again.

It was beginning to grow dark. A veil of gray deepened over the narrow red-dirt roadway, shrouding the fields that stretched away on both sides. Daphne asked, "What do they grow here? I couldn't recognize it from the train."

"Rice, *señorita*, as well as sugar cane and cotton. Don Carlos says that rice will save Louisiana." He caught her inquiring look. "Señor Osborne, the papa of your little pupil. To my master, his wife's little sons were always Carlos and Felipe even though they had no blood but the English. He was a great gentleman, Don Jaime. A true Spanish nobleman. He loved the *señora's* little ones very much."

"There were two of them?"

"*Si*, twins. Even their mother could not always tell them apart. But me, I knew. They never fooled Miguel, even when they changed their clothes for a joke. Even that Pilar"—he spat—"she could not always tell. Not even though they were children together and she grew up to marry Carlos. They were as alike as two eggs from the same nest."

"Why do you say 'were'?"

"One is dead." He touched the horse lightly with the tip of the whip. The sudden jolting as they gained speed made Daphne gasp. She sat straight, hanging onto her hat and her dignity.

They turned off the dirt road and drove in between two massive stone pillars, then down a long lane with over-arching trees at the end of which she could see a large white house. Lights gleamed dully through some of the downstairs windows, and a row of classic pillars showed ghostly white through the gathering darkness. Daphne said softly, "It's a big place."

"It was a beautiful place, *señorita*. Don Carlos' mother had it built when she married my master." The driver sketched a sign of the cross. "She was a great and beautiful lady, the Doña Camilla. Fairlawn is a copy of her home in Virginia." He broke off abruptly as they pulled up at the side of the old mansion. "Let me help you down. I myself have trained the horses to stand."

"You look after the horses?"

Miguel laughed. "I was the personal servant of Don Jaime. When he came here from his father's estate in Andalusia, I came with him, to serve him as long as we both lived. Now I am blacksmith, driver, many things. Also I guard the children with my life, if need be. Carlos and Felipe, and now the little Isabella."

Daphne followed him up the wide, low marble steps. There was no sound except the clang of their shoes on stone and the shrilling of insects in the long grass. A wide lawn dotted with neglected flower beds stretched away on three sides of the house; at some distance to the rear, outbuildings and a row of deserted slave cabins loomed through the growing dark. Pausing between two of the Corinthian pillars, she saw that they were finely finished with detailed scrolls and acanthus leaves, and then, with a feeling of disillusion, that one column was cracked, white dust drifting from the rift to the floor of the veranda.

"Enter, *señorita*."

The heavy oaken door swung shut behind them. Daphne followed the old man down a wide hall dimly lighted by single candles in wall sconces, getting a confused impression of heavy furniture and massively framed paintings as she passed. Doors stood ajar into shadowy rooms, and a mouse squeaked in the wainscot.

Miguel threw open a door. In the light of several candles, flickering in the wind from a partly-opened window, she saw three people sitting at the far end of a long oval table, their faces turned in her direction. She had a confused glimpse of heavy gleaming damask, glittering silver and, in the background, a massive sideboard of dark polished wood.

A tall slender man in work clothes got to his feet, smiling a little, and bowed. "Miss Summerfield? We've been waiting dinner for you—but perhaps you would like to go to your room before joining us?"

Pick her way through those huge shadowed corridors? Daphne said quickly, "No, thank you. Don't let me delay you further."

Could this man in rough field clothes be Mary Lee's unknown Cousin Charles? He had the gray-blue eyes and light brown hair that were so attractive in her friend, but she was tiny and dimpled and he was tall and rangy; he had a grave face, even a stern face, with an undeniable look of breeding. This was no hired hand or

11

overseer, even though he sat at the head of his table in such clothes as a field hand might wear.

Miguel said eagerly, "The new colt, he is here? All is well?"

"A beautiful filly," Charles Osborne said. The little girl at his elbow smiled at Daphne, her heart-shaped face radiant above her elaborately embroidered pinafore. She said in a clear child's voice, "Papa has promised her to me. Will you help me break her to saddle, Miguel?"

"When she is old enough. But you must care for her yourself, so she will love you and obey you."

At the master's hand sat a woman with ink-black hair piled high, glittering dark eyes in an ivory face with a knife-sharp profile. *How beautiful she is!* Daphne thought quickly. And then: *like a wild animal. A leopard, with white teeth and sharp claws.*

The woman said in a cool, clear voice, "Look after your horse, Miguel." Her black eyes met Daphne's. A chill went through the girl as she moved toward the table, where a fourth place was set and waiting. The woman's gaze was like a magnet.

She's beautiful, Daphne thought again, sinking into the chair the old servant was holding for her and shaking out the folds of an enormous serviette. She looked around the room, trying to make out its details in the dim light of the candles.

Beautiful and evil, and she hates me already. Why?

II

Lying bone-tired but unable to fall asleep in the unfamiliar four-poster, looking up at a faded silk canopy, Daphne was still thinking about Mrs. Osborne. Pilar, her husband called her. The name suited her; it had a dark mysterious sound that went well with her exotic coloring and brooding, silent beauty.

Daphne realized that although Pilar Osborne had said almost nothing to her, had in fact barely looked at her through that endless meal, she was afraid of her.

It's because she is a foreigner, she assured herself. She had never known any Spanish people. Still, the little man with the bright eyes and the deeply wrinkled face was a Spaniard, too, and she had instinctively liked and trusted him.

She was badly in need of sleep. But she was wide awake in spite of the long tiring trip and the large dinner that had been served upon her arrival. She got up quietly, pulled on the blue wool slippers that Granny had knitted for her only last Christmas, and felt along the bedside table for the candle that Suzanne had blown out after she was in bed. The silver candlestick was there, but the little enamel slipper that should have held matches was empty. She moved her hand across the table, but found only a layer of gritty dust.

Standing beside the bed in the dim light that filtered in between the heavy silk window curtains, she thought back over the evening that had just ended.

It had been a strange one. Dinner had been served by a chocolate-brown woman with a bright turban oddly knotted around her hair; she brought in course after course of unfamiliar food, served by the wavering light of wax tapers in blackened old silver holders. Many of the dishes were complex and highly seasoned. Mr. Osborne had asked a few polite questions about her journey, like a polite host trying to put a guest at ease. Mrs. Osborne—Pilar—had said nothing at all. She sat looking and remote, smoldering yet icy. It was impossible to make table talk in the face of that silent antagonism.

The little girl, Isabel, sat between her parents, eating heartily and looking at Daphne. Under other circumstances it would have been easy enough to get acquainted with her. Daphne hadn't had any trouble with the twenty or more children in the district school, even though she was a slip of seventeen when she first took her place behind the big desk and the older boys were a head taller than she was. She had kept good order and made friends with her pupils, too. Now she felt strange and helpless in the presence of one polite little girl.

Tired and timid as she was, her awe at the luxury of her surroundings lessened as the meal progressed. Obviously, the big white house with the Corinthian columns had been built by someone who had a great deal of money and a talent for spending it. The size of the dining room, the plaster cupids and swags that encircled the high ceilings, the gold-framed oil paintings hung well above eye level all bore witness to a luxurious way of living that was alien to a thrifty New Englander. But as she became accustomed to the dim light, she saw that all this richness was marred by neglect. A cobweb hung across one corner. The table was covered with heavy damask falling almost to the floor, but it had been carelessly ironed and there was a hole in her yard-square napkin. The heavy, intricately engraved knives and forks were badly tarnished. When coffee was finally served, so hot and bitter that she put the cup down after the first sip, she noticed that the eggshell-thin cup and saucer did not match.

Charles Osborne was watching her. He said quietly, "You are not accustomed to chicory in your coffee, Miss Summerfield. Let me order something else for you. A cup of tea, perhaps?"

"Oh no, this is fine." But he reached a long arm and tapped the silver bell beside his wife's plate. "Suzanne, please bring Miss Summerfield a cup of tea. How about the Lapsong Souchong that Cousin Edward Whitacre sent us?"

Pilar's profile was scornful as she took up her demitasse cup. Daphne's enjoyment of the lightly scented tea the Negress brought her was marred by a suspicion that her employer's wife already found her naïve and provincial.

The mixed impression of luxury and neglect persisted as Suzanne led the way to her bedroom, carrying a tall candle in a silver stick. The stairs, wide and curving, with a polished mahogany balustrade, had been carpeted long before in some thick soft material. Dust rose from it as they ascended, and once Daphne's heel caught in a worn spot. The bedroom into which the servant led her was full of heavy expensive-looking furniture, but the marble-topped washstand was thick with dust and the Sévres pitcher was mated with an ordinary china bowl. And now there were no matches.

For a homesick moment she let her mind dwell on Granny's little house, her home for the last twelve years. It was bare and plain, but shining with cleanliness and fragrant of beeswax polish and the lavender blossoms that Granny kept in her linen chest. She looked around her at the lowering shapes of furniture, the pale moonlight picking out garlands on the carpet. A sob rose in her throat as she remembered her own little room, where her Uncle John's daughters would be sleeping under her favorite Bonaparte's Dream quilt. And Granny lay in the churchyard beside Grampa and the two little aunts who had died before she, Daphne, was born. She was alone in the world, alone among strangers in this strange house.

Stop it, Daphne Summerfield! she told herself bravely. But two tears rolled down her cheeks. She wiped them off with the sleeve of her muslin nightgown, and blinked back the others that threatened to follow.

A high scream split the air.

Daphne jumped. A ghost? *Don't be ridiculous,* she told herself with a touch of Granny's tart New England common sense. *There aren't any ghosts.* But she stood a moment longer, too frightened to move. Where did that high, inhuman cry come from?

She tiptoed to the window, thankful that her knitted slippers and the heavy carpeting muffled her footsteps. By pulling back the heavy-brocaded curtains an inch or so she could see out. Her room was at the front of the house, directly over the long veranda and overlooking the lawn she had crossed earlier in the evening. Moonlight lay clear and white on the grass and the tangled flower beds. Black pits of shadow were under the great old trees. While she watched, something stirred under the branches and was motionless again.

She strained to see, but there was no further sign of life. A night animal, she told herself. A prowling cat, perhaps. But she was suddenly, unreasonably afraid.

She dropped the heavy curtain, suppressing a sneeze as a cloud of dust drifted up from its silken folds. She had a sudden terrified feeling that someone—or something—out there was watching her window, could see her peering out and knew she was afraid. Something that meant danger.

Then she became aware of a real danger. The window had been left halfway open. Probably Suzanne, making up the bed, had thought to give her all the fresh air possible, in this sultry Southern night. Daphne didn't blame the maid for not knowing that since the death of her parents, a dozen years before, she had walked in her sleep whenever she was very tired or emotionally upset. Granny had more than once found her on the back porch or in the garden and had gently awakened her and led her back to bed.

To fall from a second-story window would be serious, even without a marble paving below, and there was no one here to miss her and go looking for her if she wandered in the night. Frightened, she managed to tug the heavy sash down until scarcely an inch remained between it and the sill. The panes were thick and seemed to be securely fastened into the frame; she was safe, then. *I may swelter in the heat,* she thought grimly, *but at least I won't walk out of an upstairs window in my sleep. Goodness knows, I'm tired enough to.*

Back in the outsized four-poster, snuggled down between linen sheets, she was ashamed of her fears. Granny would say that she had been reading too many romantic novels.

She was half asleep when the high voice cried out again, farther away and less distinct this time. Then came a burst of sobbing, a muffled voice uttering broken words, rising in pleading. The voice of a soul in anguish, begging for help.

Closing her eyes, she told herself firmly that it was none of her business. There was nothing she could do to help. And she had a trying day ahead, the first in her new position. She was not sure what time it was, but the darkness that enfolded the room was so thick that she felt half smothered by it.

Irresistibly, she was drawn back to the window and the silvery moonlight. This time she made no attempt to find her slippers, but tiptoed cautiously across the carpet in her bare feet, careful not to stumble over any of the looming furniture.

Carefully, so that no one outside could see her —if there were really anyone out there—she pulled the curtains apart a fraction of an inch, and looked out.

A small gnomelike figure stood on the lawn in front of the house, motionless, listening. As Daphne looked out, he raised his face to her window, with a toothless smile that seemed to split his wrinkled old face.

It was Miguel.

Daphne's eyes opened wide. What was he doing there, watching the sleeping house in the middle of the night?

The sobbing and moaning had stopped. The silence was almost as frightening as the screaming had been. She found her way back to bed, wondering what was going on in the depths of the shadowy house, among the remnants of a bygone splendor.

III

"Good morning, Miss Summerfield."

Daphne sat up, blinking, not quite sure where she was. Then her eyes focused on the little girl who stood in the doorway, smiling at her. Isabel Osborne. This was the first day in her new post, and she was at Fairlawn. She managed to return the smile, brushing away the memories of the night's confusion and disturbance.

"We brought your breakfast," Isabel said in her high sweet voice. "It's all right, Suzanne. She's awake."

The stout Negress who had waited on the table the previous evening walked smoothly into the room, carrying a tray covered with dishes and little silver domes. She said nothing, but beamed at Daphne as she removed the candlestick and empty match holder from the night table and arranged the tray in their place. Then she went to the window and pulled the long tasseled cord that hung down beside the sash. The heavy curtains parted, letting in a flood of sunshine. Daphne blinked in the sudden radiance.

Isabel perched on a tufted slipper chair. "Suzanne let me make your tea all by myself," she said proudly. The servant smiled again and silently withdrew, closing the door behind her. "I thought I had better come along," Isabel explained seriously. Her face now reminded Daphne of her father's. "Suzanne can't talk, you see. She hears everything, but she has never been able to speak, not even when she was a little girl."

Daphne didn't know what answer to make. Isabel chattered on. "Anyway, she's been in the family ever since she was born, so it doesn't matter much. She was a little girl when *Mamacita* brought her here from Virginia—you know, my papa's mother, the Doña Camilla. If you want anything, all you have to do is tell Suzanne and she will take care of it for you."

"Does she do the cooking, too?" For the fragrance of crisp bacon, hot biscuit and a spicy jam was creeping out from underneath the silver covers. *Well*, Daphne thought, repressing a giggle, *I've read about high-born ladies having breakfast in bed, but not governesses.*

"She does everything. We used to have a lot of servants," Isabel said chattily, "but the others all went away after *Mamacita* died. That was before I was born, but Miguel has told me all about it. Suzanne helped to take care of my papa when he was a little boy, and so did Miguel, just as they helped take care of me."

Daphne considered this, buttering her first roll. One woman to do all the work in this big house—a mansion, really, with its huge rooms, high ceilings and abundance of heavily carved furniture. No wonder everything was dilapidated and dusty. But the food was excellent, piping hot and carefuly seasoned, and she pushed back all the questions that rose to the surface of her mind. She asked casually, "Why does she wear that cloth on her head?"

"The tignon?" Isabel sounded surprised. "But they all do, the Negroes here. It shows that she's a house servant. Is it different in Maine?"

"Most of us do our own work," Daphne said dryly. She thought that the house would be beautiful if it were cleaned and aired, the furniture polished and put in order. *I might begin with my own room*, she told herself. Isabel ought to learn something about making a home, too, no matter what the custom here may be.

It was apparent that, however wealthy and prominent the Osbornes might have been in the past, they had come down in the world. Or was there some other reason why this huge establishment was looked after by a single servant, and she an outsider, born into the family? Was there a reason why the local people wouldn't go into service here? A mute aging woman to do the work of an entire domestic staff, a superstitious old gnome in charge of the stables, and the cold proud Pilar for a mistress—no wonder things were run-down! The magnitude of the problem overwhelmed her. She reminded herself hastily that it wasn't her problem. She was responsible ony for Isabel.

The little girl was talking happily. "I'll take your tray to the kitchen when you are through with it. Then I'll show you Fairlawn. We needn't have any lessons today. Papa says so. You can come and see my little new filly."

At least the child was friendly, and the combination of morning sunshine and a good breakfast made Daphne a little ashamed of the night's forebodings. She had dreaded meeting Pilar at the breakfast table. But of course, Continental ladies had their breakfast in bed. She had read about it in the novels Granny deplored.

The air in the room was heavy and humid. She asked, "Is it always this hot?"

"Only in the summer," the child said seriously. "You ought to have your window open, and a new mosquito bar for your bed. Shall I open it for you?"

Daphne tried to laugh. "You see, I sometimes walk in my sleep. You don't want me to walk out of an upstairs window, do you?"

Isabel was right: it was very hot, with an oppressive humidity that threatened to be worse later in the day. After the child left, carefully balancing the tray, she put on one of the cotton dresses she had worn in schoolroom on hot spring days, and arranged her golden-brown curls in a neat pompadour. She surveyed the results in a gilt-framed pier glass that stood, spotty and tarnished but still elegant, in a corner of the room. She looked too young, and—yes, she might as well admit it—too pretty to inspire awe in a pupil. Already, little curls were breaking loose from her hairpins. If only she were tall and stately! Isabel, at ten, was almost as tall as she was.

She found her way down the wide stairs, able to appreciate by daylight what she had only guessed at the night before, the grace of the wide curving steps and the beautiful balustrade. The dust and neglect showed, too, but they didn't seem quite so important in the cheerful morning light.

At the foot of the stairs she hesitated, unsure which of the heavy paneled doors to try. The lower hall was really a room, furnished with heavy chairs and tables and hung with dim paintings. A little spinet piano stood against one wall, a delicate wreath of roses painted above the yellowed keys, looking light and frivolous among so much carved mahogany and cherrywood. The floor was laid out in big squares of black and white marble, crisscrossed with dusty footprints. Above one door a pair of swords were crossed. On impulse, she pushed against the heavy iron bar that looked as if it could repel an invading army when dropped into an equally

23

massive lock. This must be the main entrance to the house, she thought; and she was right. The heavy panel of oak swung out. She found herself on the long veranda she had crossed the night before. Isabel, leaning against a cracked pillar with a kitten in her lap, jumped up and dropped a sketchy curtsy.

"Come on, I'll show you everything." Isabel stopped, frowning. "Well, not really everything. I'm not allowed to go in the fields unless Papa takes me, and never, never to the bayou. There are quicksands in the bayou. And alligators that can kill people." Her eyes widened with excitement. "There used to be smugglers, too, in the olden days."

"It sounds exciting."

"Papa will take us some time. I'll ask him to take us to Hidden Island for a picnic, when he has time. That's where he and Tio Felipe used to play when they were little boys. My papa knows every inch of the bayou like his own back yard. That's what he says."

She took Daphne's hand in her hard little paw. "Come on, I'll show you the horses. The new one that was born yesterday belongs to me; did you know that? Miguel will break her for me to ride when she's old enough." Her face clouded. "Only that will be four years, and I'll be a young lady by that time."

Daphne smiled, even though four years sounded almost as long to her as it did to Isabel. "You can take care of her while you wait. Then she'll love you more than anybody; do you see?"

The stables were within shouting distance of the big house. She decided as she followed Miguel from stall to stall that they were looked after better than the house. Most of the compartments stood empty, the names of their former occupants neatly printed on cards above the mangers. But there were four good saddle horses, including Isabel's Bluebird, and they were all in top condition. Everything was swept clean, and the pleasant fragrance of leather, grain and horses hung over it all. "We will have a racing stable again—if my master is right about the rice," Miguel told her. "And this is where I live, *señorita*."

He had swept the harness room clean and furnished it with an old armchair, a narrow cot and a few rough shelves. Daphne supposed that he slept here to be near the horses. As though reading her mind, he shook his head. "The air is clean here. There are evil things in that house—spells and secrets—things that hurt." He looked at Isabel and shook his head slightly. "Do not be afraid, Miguel watches always."

Daphne thought uncomfortably of the strange happenings in the night: the screams and moans, the little man standing in the middle of the lawn keeping watch over the house. She wandered over to his work bench, covered with tools she could not recognize but as orderly as the array of egg beaters and mixing spoons in Granny's kitchen cupboard. "What is this?" she asked, looking at a metal contraption with several deep depressions in it.

"A bullet mold, *señorita*. The father of Doña Camilla carried this gun in the War Between the States—and with this, he cast his bullets." He picked up a clumsy-looking weapon and handed it to her. She saw that most of the rust had been carefully polished away and the moving parts oiled. "But will it shoot? After all this time?"

"Who knows? I amuse myself with this plaything in the evenings when I have nothing better to do." He pulled open a small drawer in the work table. A dozen or so rough-cast, blunt-nosed pieces of metal lay there. "When I have polished these, then we will see."

Isabel said seriously, "Sometimes a vulture gets after the chickens."

Miguel chuckled. "There are plenty of guns on this place that will do for the vultures! Do not worry about my playthings, *chiquita*. Do I come to the house and play with your dolls?"

Daphne's quick eye caught a bright gleam in the corner of the drawer. Impulsively, she reached for it. The slug was the same shape and size as the others, but lighter and brighter. It shone purely in the morning sunshine.

Miguel's face grew stern. He took the object from her, put it back in the drawer, and looked intently into her face. What he saw there reassured him. "Pure silver. I made it from a Spanish coin that my godmother gave me at my christening."

"But why?"

A shadow fell across the clean-swept floor. The three of them turned like puppets on a single string: the old man, the young teacher, the little girl. At the sight of the woman who stood there,

26

all the smiles vanished. Miguel stepped nimbly to one side so that his body concealed the open drawer. *"Buenas días, Doña Pilar."*

Pilar Osborne said in her voice that was at once musical and cold, "If you have nothing better to do than to keep Miguel from his work, you might as well be in the schoolroom. Come with me, Miss Summerfield. I will show you the house and garden. There is nothing to interest you here."

IV

"Four sixes are twenty-four," Isabel said confidently, "and five sixes are thirty, and six sixes are thirty-six." She took a deep breath and looked hopefully at her father. He nodded. "Go on."

"Seven sixes are forty-five. No, that's not right." She put her hands behind her back. Charles Osborne said gravely, "No fair counting on your fingers. Start over if you need to."

"I know, forty-two." She gave him a questioning look. "Eight sixes?" he suggested gently.

"Forty-eight, and nine sixes are fifty-four! I do know it, Papa."

"You're doing quite well, I think." He scooped her into his arms and looked over her bright curls at Daphne. "Both of you deserve a holiday. Why don't we take the rest of the day off and have a picnic?"

It seemed to Daphne that they had had a great many holidays, but she had to admit that Isabel learned quickly, even if she was far behind ten-year-olds in Maine. Equally important, she had a sunny nature and remained friendly even if her teacher felt obliged to scold her or make her do an assignment over. No one seemed to have taken a systematic interest in her education, and she regarded lessons as a delightful game. There were moments when Daphne felt the same way. Indeed, at the end of her first month at Fairlawn she had been almost reluctant to accept the gold pieces and bank notes her employer put into her hand. But the child's progress eased her conscience. With only one pupil, and that one both bright and affectionate, she could cover in two or three hours the lessons that would have taken a whole day if Isabel had been in an ordinary school among other children.

Osborne said, "I have a free half-day myself. Don't you think I deserve a picnic, Miss Summerfield?"

She couldn't help returning his smile. He stood there in the rough field clothes he wore even on Sundays, tall and lanky, serious as always but with a twinkle in his eyes. She said primly, "If you say so, Mr. Osborne."

"Oh, Papa, can we go to the island?"

"Not this time, *chiquita*. A buyer is coming this afternoon to look at the rice, so we must be back. It takes a whole day for the island, you know."

"Then the cemetery. Please, Papa!"

Daphne's eyes widened. Charles Osborne laughed. "It's not as bad as it sounds, Miss Summerfield. A Louisiana cemetery is not a mournful place—in fact, on All Saints it's customary to picnic there. A sort of family reunion! But we don't sit on the graves with our bread and butter; we visit the family vault first and then have our picnic luncheon in a nearby grove, as the country people hereabouts do. This young lady won't be satisfied until she has introduced you to her ancestors."

It was a new idea to Daphne, but she was inclined to agree with anything her employer proposed. "After all, we used to play in the burying ground when we were children. Shall I ask Suzanne to prepare sandwiches?"

"Oh, she'll have something much better than sandwiches in store for us! Tell her, by all means. You get along well with Suzanne, don't you?"

"She's very nice," Daphne assured him. "It troubled me at first that I couldn't talk with her, but now it doesn't really matter. We understand each other without words."

He laughed. "Better than you would if she could converse with you, no doubt. I don't know what the local dialect grafted on a Virginian accent would sound like, but nothing like the speech of a Maine hired girl, I can assure you. I don't suppose you would be afraid to try it, though."

"She isn't afraid of anything," Isabel assured him. " 'Cept walking out of her window in the middle of the night, because she walks in her sleep sometimes."

"Is that so? Then we must have safeguards

put on your window, Miss Summerfield, like the ones in the nursery. Isabel doesn't need them any longer. I'll ask Miguel to move them."

Daphne felt her cheeks reddening with embarrassment. "Please don't bother. Isabel is exaggerating." She searched hurriedly for another subject. "Will Mrs. Osborne go with us?"

"I'll ask her." He untangled himself from Isabel's arms. "Go and wash your inky fingers, *chiquita*, and see if you can help Suzanne. Miss Summerfield is right when she says that a young lady should know her way around the kitchen as well as the parlor. My mother believed that, too, and always washed her fine china and silver no matter how many servants she commanded."

Daphne tried to repress an unkind hope that Mrs. Osborne would choose to stay home. In the six weeks since her arrival at Fairlawn, she and Isabel had become close friends. She felt at ease with Isabel's father, even though they met only at mealtime and when he dropped into the schoolroom, as today, to see how the lessons were coming along. But the proud Pilar was another matter. She was always courteous, but she was as much a stranger to Daphne as on the night of their first meeting, and she made it clear that she wanted it that way.

More, it was impossible to like her. *I don't know what it is,* Daphne thought helplessly as she brushed her hair in front of the tarnished pier glass. *I feel as though she'd like to hurt me. As though she resented and hated everybody. Yet I've never heard her say a sharp word.*

She was unreasonably disappointed to find Pilar, slender and erect in ruffled white, waiting on the veranda when Miguel brought the surrey around. After all, she reminded herself, it's her house and her family. Or her husband's. On an impulse, she asked, "Are your relatives buried in Saint Laurent Parish, too, Mrs. Osborne?"

Pilar's eyes narrowed. "Certainly. Don Jaime Ramirez y Molinaro was only the stepfather of Carlos and Felipe, but he was my own father. That did not change when he married the Doña Camilla and adopted her two sons. We grew up as sister and brothers." She smiled thinly. 'Until we were grown, and Carlos fell in love with me." She looked both bitter and self-satisfied, and her husband, perched beside Miguel, gave no sign that he had heard.

Daphne thought about their relationship all the way to the burying ground, forgetting to look at the unfamiliar countryside except when Isabel politely pointed out some feature of special interest.

The cemetery itself, located on the edge of the small town of Saint Laurent, was unlike anything she had ever seen before. Instead of grassy mounds planted with shrubs and flowers, and set off by granite headstones, there were stone and marble vaults built above ground and ornamented with carved crosses, angels and doves as well as the names of the deceased. "The dead are inside," Osborne explained, seeing her bewilderment. "You see, the earth here is marshy. It floods easily. So we bury our dead above ground."

She privately thought that the vaults were ostentatious and ugly, but she followed the others across stretches of clay soil and stopped when they did to read the names of relatives and family friends deeply carved into the walls that sheltered their bones. Angelique and Victorine D'Estienne. Edouard Toussaint Jourdain. Francisco Ricardo Rodriguez y Chavez. And on the largest and most elaborate structure of all, with a winged angel in bas-relief as well as a lily-twined cross, the name Pilar had uttered so proudly: Don Jaime Ramirez y Molinaro, with his wife alongside, Doñ Camilla Osborne de Ramirez.

Charles Osborne took off his wide-brimmed hat and sketched the sign of the cross. "My parents."

"My father." Pilar's voice was cold steel.

Isabel looked from one to the other. This struggle for family precedence was apparently an old story to her. Old Miguel, standing respectfully behind his employers, muttered something. Pilar turned to look at him.

Charles said cheerfully, "Right. My own father is buried with his kinfolks in Virginia, but I can't remember him. My mother was a widow with two noisy dirty-handed little boys when Don Jaime married her. A brave man!" His smile vanished. "And my brother is buried in Spain."

Miguel bowed his head. Pilar's lips tightened. Charles Osborne said to Isabel, "Now are you satisfied? Have you paid your respects to your ancestors? Can you think about ordinary things like cold chicken and jam cake?"

"Oh, Papa!"

"Since this was your idea, you can help Miguel carry the hampers to the grove. It will give you an appetite. Not that yours is ever lacking."

"I'll help, too." Daphne hurried after Miguel, glad to escape from the couple who stood before the family mausoleum. There was something electric in the air, like the uneasy hush before a thunderstorm. It was a relief to start unpacking supplies from the carriage, which had been left just outside the wrought-iron gates of the cemetery. She took charge with unusual brusqueness.

The old servant bustled around, muttering angrily. "She—the daughter of Don Jaime! The spawn of the gypsy camp, and only her mother's lying word to go by! Don Jaime was a Spanish gentleman of the highest rank, not for such as her to mention. Yes, at home he bore a title. And that witch—"

Daphne cut him off. "Hand me the big basket, please, Miguel. It's time for lunch."

"*Bueno, bueno, señorita.* Only remember what I say. The woman is a witch. Do not take anything that hers. She can do you great harm."

"Do you mean Isabel?" Privately, she thought that the relation between the child and her mother was more like that of strangers living in the same house. If her young pupil responded to affection from an outsider, whose fault was it?

"No, not Isabel." He fell silent as the little girl came panting up to them, eager to help. "Is there roast chicken Miguel? Is there mushroom paste in the rolls?"

33

He nodded. "And strawberries, and the little shrimp you like so well. Suzanne has made a good luncheon for you."

But Daphne was too puzzled to enjoy the delicious food, when it was finally spread out on a long table in the grove that adjoined the cemetery. She took the plate her pupil handed her, but she hardly tasted the sweet little strawberries or the tarragon-flavored chicken. She was trying to piece together the history of two oddly assorted people, Isabel's parents.

They had been foster brother and sister, brought up together—and had married, apparently, before they were old enough to know the meaning of love. Isabel had showed her their marriage certificate, framed on the wall of the library, and she had been startled to find that Charles Osborne was barely thirty years old. He had the grave and thoughtful bearing of an older man, perhaps because he always looked tired. Brought up in luxury, he toiled in the rice fields like a hired hand, putting in as long a day as the Negroes who worked for wages, and carrying, in addition, all of the worry and responsibility. If the fields were not flooded properly after the seedlings were set out, if it were too wet or too dry, all his work would be wasted and the debts that burdened Fairlawn would mount still higher.

She knew from Miguel that he was struggling to bring Fairlawn back to its former prosperity. He had pioneered with rice growing in a country mostly planted in cane and cotton. This was the kind of ambition a girl brought up on the rocky coasts of New England could understand and admire.

Pilar, on the other hand, did not work at all. If she went to the kitchen, it was to give orders to the silent Suzanne, who thereafter did just as she pleased. She seemed not to notice that the tables were thick with dust and the brocaded sofas ripped, that cobwebs hung from the ceilings and the fine old oil paintings were dimmed with dirt and time. She took no more interest in her child's upbringing. Isabel's clothes were looked after and her curls brushed by Suzanne, who, like Miguel, was devoted to the child. Pilar spent most of the day in her room. She arranged her jet-black hair, ate candy, played the mandolin and lay on the chaise longue smoking cigarette after cigarette, her eyes narrowed against the smoke. Daphne had never seen a woman smoke before. But perhaps, she thought, it was customary among gypsies.

She decided, feeling unreasonably depressed by the realization, that they must have loved each other, at least when they were younger. From the novels Granny deplored and her own observation of the neighbors back home, she knew that even marriages built on passionate love sometimes turned out badly.

There was another detail of the family history that puzzled her. She managed to ask Miguel about it a few days after the visit to the cemetery. Isabel had taken her colt out into the paddock and was grooming it while Daphne perched on the kitchen chair Miguel kept for his infrequent visitors. "Miguel, you told me that Mr. Osborne had a twin brother."

"*Si.*"

"Why is he buried in Spain? Did he go there to live after his stepfather was buried?"

Miguel looked around cautiously. The child was out of earshot, crooning to her little horse as she combed the tangles out of its mane. "They grew up here, the three of them. Carlos and Pilar married young—gypsies grow up, *señorita*, earlier than civilized people, and that one tricked him into marriage."

Daphne looked away. She had compared the date on the marriage certificate with that of Isabel's birth, and it made her think less of Charles Osborne.

"Felipe was not happy with the marriage, but he stayed to help with the plantation. You will understand that after Don Jaime and Doña Camilla were gone, there was little money left. It was the dream of both brothers to restore the plantation and make an inheritance for the little Isabel."

"And then—"

"The brother of Don Jaime passed away, on his estate near Granada. There was talk of an inheritance. You must know that Don Jaime had made these children his own according to the American law, with papers from the court. Felipe was to go to the home of their ancestors and present their claim, since he was the older by an hour. But Pilar was not happy with this. Perhaps she feared that he would find some way to cheat her. After all, *señorita,* she was Don Jaime's own daughter, but born out of wedlock, you understand, so that she had no claim to his patrimony. She wanted to be sure that Carlos would have his half of the estate. He must go with his brother."

"And did he?"

Miguel looked stern. "There was never a greater gentleman or a more honest man than Don Felipe Ramirez y Osborne. It was he who loved this land with a deep love, and who sought for a way to build the family fortunes again. More, he loved the little Isabel like his own child. Even if he had married and had sons, he would not have robbed her of his inheritance."

"But what happened?" Daphne persisted.

"There was a railway accident in the mountains near Cordoba. One died. He was buried with the ancestors of his foster parent. The other came home to Fairlawn, alone."

"What happened to the inheritance?"

Miguel shrugged. "*Nada.* Nothing left but the title, and who in this country wears a title? Further, Carlos and Felipe were not of the blood. They could not have inherited it. Of the money, nothing was left. Even the acres had been sold to pay the uncle's debts."

Daphne sighed. "It's a romantic story, anyway."

"And a sad one. He who came back moved all of his possessions into the room he and his brother had shared in their youth. He locks the door at night," Miguel said with a sudden grin.

"Do not be frightened, *señorita*, if you hear strange sounds in the house at night. Even a witch cannot fly through keyholes. Not when the key is turned from the other side."

V

"Good night, Pilar. Good night, Miss Summerfield. You look a little pale. I hope you have no trouble sleeping these hot nights."

Conscious of Pilar's eyes, Daphne could only murmur, "Thank you." She didn't want to tell her employer that, so far from making her wakeful, the heavy, humid weather induced a lassitude which made it difficult to remain awake through the many courses of dinner. She suspected that he found all this formal service a burden, too. In spite of his courtly manners, she was sharply conscious of his constant fatigue. As an outsider, she had no right to be concerned about a condition that his own wife found not worth mentioning, unless one were to take her occasional irritable comments as a sign of anxiety.

She knew that Charles was up at daybreak and in the fields before anyone else was stirring, except the loyal and hard-working Suzanne. He came to the big house for a hasty lunch at midday, and was back at work before the hands had finished their noonday rest. In this climate it was considered dangerous to work in the midday sun, for black as well as white; the helpers stretched out under a convenient tree or sheltered in one of the abandoned slave cabins through the worst part of the day, having been in the fields since sunrise.

But for the plantation owner, struggling to recover the family fortunes, there was no rest. Charles came to the dinner table every night in fresh work clothes, courteous but too tired for small talk. Daphne secretly found herself wishing she could lighten his labors. If his wife were only a little more concerned about him—

She reminded herself that the relations of her pupil's father with his wife were none of her business. She was an outsider in this house.

Tonight she was more than glad to retire to her room as soon as dinner was over. The spicy food, the oppressive heat and the feeling of foreboding that hung over Fairlawn made it difficult to keep from nodding while the others sipped their hot bitter coffee. She made her way slowly up the thickly carpeted stairs, looked into Isabel's room, where the child lay smiling in her sleep, and reached her own room with a feeling of relief.

It seemed less sultry here than downstairs. In order not to disperse the coolness she undressed in the dark, washed her face in the tepid water from the china pitcher, and got into bed. Drowsiness enfolded her almost before she fastened down her mosquito net. Too late, she remembered that she hadn't read her customary chapter from the Bible. She began to repeat a familiar Psalm as she felt herself relaxing, but the words blurred in her mind and she realized that she was tired to the point of exhaustion. *Never mind,* she thought, smiling in the dark as the words began to tangle. *God will forgive me, I'm sure.*

In her dream she was a child again, walking on the beach. A cool wind blew off the Atlantic, fragrant of salt and seaweed. *I'd like to go wading,* she thought. *Granny won't mind; it's low tide.* She took a step forward and stood poised over the shallow water. There was a shriek—a gull or a human voice, she couldn't be sure. She stood balanced on one foot, listening.

And awoke.

She was standing on the low broad sill of her room at Fairlawn, leaning over the marble-paved veranda which glimmered up at her through the dark. Another step, and she would have hurtled down into darkness.

Suppressing a scream, she threw herself backward and landed in a heap on the thick carpet. A sharp pain flashed through her foot and ankle, but she ignored it. Still confused with sleep, she lay looking up at the window. It was wide open, the curtain pulled aside. The square of sky showed almost as dark as the air inside the room, for it was the dark of the moon, but the wind blew in and ruffled her hair. Now she remembered noticing the freshness and fragrance of the night air while she was undressing. There could be no doubt that someone had opened her window during the evening, between the time when she freshened up for dinner and the hour of her drowsy retiring.

Suzanne? But the housekeeper had been grateful when Daphne took over the care of her own room, giving it a thorough New England housecleaning and then putting it in order every morning. She was equally pleased when the young governess announced that in the future, she and Isabel would take their breakfast in the little morning room adjoining the kitchen, rather than the gloomy dining room. The silent servant had more work than she could do, since she took the place of the staff of trained servants that had looked after the big house in Camilla Ramirez's day.

Suzanne, of course, might still have opened the window for fresh air, not knowing that Daphne had a habit of walking in her sleep. Only Isabel knew that. And Charles. Daphne sat up dizzily as realization struck her. She remembered the conversation in the schoolroom, the day of the picnic. Isabel would never have opened the window; she was too aware of her teacher's danger, and she was too warm and loving a child to plan harm, as well as too transparent to keep even an innocent secret.

Only one other person in this house knew why she opened her window a mere crack on these sultry nights, preferring peace of mind to bodily comfort. Isabel had told her father, and he had immediately seemed concerned. Had wanted to take the protective bars off the nursery windows and put them on hers, for her safety.

Why didn't I let him? she thought as an inadvertent move made her injured ankle hurt again. And then: *is it possible that he did this?*

The idea was so fantastic that she rejected it almost before it was formed. Charles Osborne a murderer, that kind and gentle man who worked fifteen hours a day to restore his little daughter's partimony? And if he had been capable of such a deed, what grudge could he hold against her?

She realized that she was lying on her bedroom floor and that the window was wide open, exposing her to the gaze of anyone who might be lurking among the great trees. In spite of the almost tropical heat, she shivered. Who, or what, was watching from the silence?

She got carefully to her feet, putting as little weight as possible on the injured ankle and trying to stay out of direct range of the open window. She managed to grasp the silk cord that held the draperies and pull them shut; and then, hidden by folds of material, to pull the sash down almost to the sill. She was risking no second sleepwalking episode tonight!

It was an accident. I left it open when I finished putting the room in order, this morning.

But she distinctly remembered closing it. The curtain pull stuck, and she had made a mental note to ask Suzanne for some wax for the frayed cord.

Then Suzanne or Isabel simply opened it and forgot it. A simple accident.

Of course, that was the reasonable explanation. Stupid accidents happened because people were careless.

Reassured, she got back into bed, feeling safer even though the ankle was beginning to hurt more than she had expected it to.

She was half asleep when the noises started. A wild scream, followed by loud sobbing, and then a spate of muffled words.

This time there was no doubt where it came from. The excitement was down the hall, and it was unmistakably human. She had never heard Pilar's voice raised above chill displeasure, but this hysterical frenzy was unmistakably hers. "But why, why? Why do you do this to me? No man treats his wife like this. Please, please stop tormenting me. I tell you I cannot bear this torture any longer!"

Daphne strained to hear the reply, but there was none.

Pilar's voice grew sharper. "I tell you I am afraid of you! Do you hear me? You are crazy! You have been crazy ever since Felipe was killed! *Tu es loco, loco, loco!*"

VI

By daybreak her ankle was swollen and discolored, and the pain was worse. She got out of bed and managed to dress, running through Granny's list of home remedies as she tried in vain to insert her puffy foot in a shoe. Hot water, an oatmeal poultice, flaxseed to draw the swelling out? Perhaps, she thought hopefully, Suzanne would know of something. The old woman had a large store of practical wisdom, and nothing ever seemed to alarm or disturb her.

She put on her knitted slippers and limped down the hall as quietly as she could in order not to wake the sleeping family. The stairs looked endless. The pain was coming in sharp waves now; she pressed her lips together to keep from crying out. With a nostalgic thought of Granny's neat little house, where everything was in easy reach, she managed the first step and then the second. *I'd like to slide down the banister,* she thought with a nervous giggle. It wasn't really funny, though. She stopped, clinging to catch her breath before going on again.

"What's the matter?"

Charles stood at the foot of the stairs, looking up. For a moment the fright of the previous night flooded through her, a physical sensation. Then reason reasserted itself. There couldn't possibly be anything sinister about the tall, serious-faced man who stood there with a steaming cup in his hand, waiting for her answer.

"I fell. I'm sorry, but I think my ankle is sprained." She tried to keep her tone light, but new pain shot through her foot and she trailed off in a ragged gasp. "I thought perhaps a hot poultice?"

Osborne said curtly, "Don't move." Before she knew what was happening, he ran lightly up the long curving flight of stairs and picked her up as easily as though she had been a small child. "No, don't talk."

A sweet relief filled her. She closed her eyes and rested her head against his chest. He carried her to the foot of the stairs, through the little morning room where the table was set for her and Isabel's breakfast, and into the kitchen where he set her down gently in Suzanne's old rocking chair. "It's a good thing you are a small girl. If you weighed as much as Suzanne you might still be standing at the top of the stairs."

Daphne giggled. The kitchen was aromatic with freshly roasted coffee; sunshine and the fragrance of summer flowers came in through the open back door. Suzanne turned from the cook-stove, her face shocked and concerned. Charles gently removed the slipper and then, in spite of her protests, her stocking, and looked at the swollen ankle.

In the honest morning light it was impossible to believe that last night had really happened. It seemed like a bad dream. But there was the injury to prove that those sobs and accusations had really sounded through the upstairs.

Charles said, "I don't think it's broken, but you won't be walking on it for a while. What happened?"

"I fell getting out of bed."

"We'd better let a doctor see it. Dr. Perron at Saint Laurent is a remarkably good man for a small town—stays there because it's where his widowed mother lives, not to mention a million or so other relatives. He's the closest, too. I'll have Miguel hitch the bay to the light buggy."

"Miguel has enough to do without taking me to the doctor."

"True. I'll take you myself."

"But, Mr. Osborne!"

Charles was out of the house before she could make any further protest. Suzanne, smiling, was

45

at her elbow with a cup of the fine imported tea she prepared every morning. Daphne took it gratefully. "Thank you, Suzanne. I don't really need to see a doctor. I'm sure a hot pack will be enough."

Suzanne's shrug and rolling eyes conveyed as plainly as words could have done that Mr. Charles was in charge of the situation and would make the decisions. Daphne smiled and nodded. It was hardly fair to argue with a woman who couldn't talk back, although Suzanne seldom had any trouble making herself understood without the use of words.

Besides, she was beginning to agree that it might be just as well to let this Dr. Perron, whoever he was, look at her foot. It was certainly becoming more painful. Suppose it were broken, after all?

It would be good to see someone not connected with Fairlawn, too. Her spirits rose when at last she was perched beside her employer on the high seat of the light carriage. She looked eagerly at the fields as they rolled by, at the little cabins half hidden by clumps of unfamiliar trees. It was weeks since she had seen anyone who wasn't a part of the plantation. She had read about the gaiety and open-handed hospitality of Southern life, but the Osbornes seemed not to have any neighbors: no one paid calls on Pilar, although many of the gentry roundabout were of Spanish descent, and Isabel's only playmates were the horses and a never-ending supply of barn cats. Charles rode into town once a week to pick up the mail and replenish such supplies as were needed by their small household. She had seen the field hands only at a distance.

At first she had been fascinated by the unfamiliar and, to her, exotic details of her new life, then engrossed by Isabel's personality and the challenge of setting up a routine for the little girl's days. Then the strange and disturbing happenings of the nights had shut out all wonder about the neighboring countryside. Now she realized that she was lonely. At home, Granny and the neighbors had always been close at hand, even when the snow lay deep on the country roads and the winter wind cut like a well-sharpened knife. If you were snowed in you were at least snowed in with people you knew, understood, and trusted.

Now she was locked in a strange place with a man who was hardly ever in the house, a child —loving and bright, but still a child—and a woman who preferred her own company to all others and spent endless days doing nothing, apparently in perfect content.

Really, she thought, *Miguel and Suzanne are the only friends I have.* A speechless woman and an old man lost in brooding as he busied himself with looking after the animals and doing a multitude of small tasks around the place.

She remembered Pilar's caustic remarks about neighbors who insisted on speaking only French after four generations in Louisiana. She asked timidly, "Does he speak English?"

Charles came out of his revery. "Perron? Quite good English, as well as French, German, Spanish and, I suppose, Latin and Greek. He graduated from Harvard University a few years before I did. Are you looking for someone to confide in?"

"I haven't anything to confide," Daphne said primly. Did he look relieved or was she imagining it?

Suddenly she saw her situation as it might have appeared to another person. She was driving on a remote country road with a man she scarcely knew, a man whose wife accused him, with midnight shrieks and sobbing, of being mad. She was a stranger in the neighborhood, without friends or refuge. And just now—the realization of her helplessness came home to her—she was unable to walk without support, even to get out of the buggy unaided. She had heard of girls who disappeared under just such circumstances.

It was true, too, that people could brood over their troubles until they became irrational, and then break into violent actions of which they would not ordinarily be capable. If the loss of his brother and the weight of his financial problems, coming at the same time, had become a heavier load than he could carry; if the mysterious quarrel with his wife that kept him from sharing her room had erupted into open hostility; if, above all, the injuries he had suffered on the train wreck were more serious than the doctor realized—then, she supposed, his reason might be slipping.

He was pale, and there were tired lines around his mouth and eyes. *I don't believe it!* she thought with a sudden lifting of her spirits. This was a man who could be deeply hurt. She didn't think he could hurt others.

Still, she was glad when they reached Saint Laurent. It was a sleepy little hamlet, the only people in sight being three scraggy old men whittling on a bench in front of the general store and a fat woman with a market basket over her arm. There was also a rawboned hound asleep in the middle of the dusty road. But Dr. Perron was in his office above the store, which was the post office as well. He came running down the outside stairs to greet them, a thin brown-faced man with bright brown eyes and a warm smile. He unwrapped the ankle at once, to Daphne's embarrassment, and made a clucking noise. "Mrs. Jackson would not want you to climb all those stairs, and indeed it would be impossible for you, mademoiselle. Let us go into the room behind the store. I have used it as a consulting room in many emergencies." He turned to Charles. "Do you remember, *mon ami,* that I set a broken arm for you before I was legally entitled to practice? I had learned from watching my father—always my best teacher."

"No, that was—" Charles stopped short. "Yes, of course I remember. Got thrown trying to break the gray stallion—I thought I was a cowboy in a Wild West show. We were both old enough to know better."

The room behind the store was pleasantly cool and smelled of coffee beans and yard goods. Mrs. Jackson came in, the storekeeper's wife, a stout motherly woman who adopted Daphne on sight and brought coffee to all of them as soon as the bandaging was finished; Daphne managed to drink hers, aware that Charles was watching her with amusement. Covered with a spicy-smelling ointment and snugly bandaged, the foot felt better and after an exchange of polite remarks she was able to hop back to the street, leaning on the wiry little doctor. The two men boosted her to the high seat as though she had been a rag doll. Perron said seriously, "You'll never get her down again, Charles, without my help."

"She's no great weight, André."

She felt herself blushing under the doctor's politely inquiring gaze.

They were well outside the village before Charles spoke again. "I should have asked if you wanted anything from the store."

"Why, I don't believe so."

"There is nothing much there. Pilar turns up her nose at the thought of buying even a needle or a spool of thread from the village," he said lightly, "and as for a bottle of scent or a piece of lace, it's not worth looking at unless it comes from New Orleans. I must admit there's little here to tempt a lady."

Daphne said with sudden boldness, "I am not a lady, Mr. Osborne. I am a governess with her living to earn."

He turned to her. "I think you are very much a lady, Miss Summerfield. You are kind and brave and—loving, I should think."

50

She looked away, feeling the color rise in her face and the sudden sting of tears in her eyes.

He said, "Forgive me. I had no right to say that."

I could be loving, she answered him silently as they jolted over the rutted country road. *If the right man cared for me, and I for him—if we were free to love each other. I could be gentle and affectionate, not selfish and bad-tempered like some women.*

She reminded herself that these thoughts were suitable to neither her station in life nor her present circumstances, with another woman's husband at her side. It would be well to think of something else. But further conversation seemed impossible. She was silent all the way back to Fairlawn, wrapped in her own thoughts. Charles, too, seemed lost in meditation.

Miguel was waiting for them between the great gatepost when they turned off the road. His face was a mask of fury and grief. At the sight of him, Charles pulled the horses to a sharp stop. He leaned over and asked something in a language Daphne couldn't understand. The little groom burst into a spate of excited talk.

Daphne asked anxiously, "Has something happened to Isabel?"

"Heartbreak, *señorita.* Her little colt is dead."

"But how!"

Miguel shrugged. "I am having a small black in the kitchen, as I always do in the middle of the morning." He glanced at Charles, who nodded. "Suddenly comes the *niña* screaming and in

51

tears. She has gone as always to feed and water the little horse. It lies dead in the stall."

Charles asked grimly, "From what cause?"

"There is not a mark on it, master. I think the evil eye."

"Why? The creature hasn't harmed anyone, and God knows it's not in Isabel to bring such a punishment on herself. It was done to hurt her, of course; the filly was hers and she loved it, but why?"

"Perhaps in the senselessness of rage," the old man said. "Perhaps to hurt you through the child."

Daphne shuddered.

Charles said white-faced, "So help me, I'd kill anyone who hurt Isabel. If I could be sure—"

Miguel put a shaky hand on the horse's mane. The animal looked at him with quiet trust. "I also, *amigo*. Only be careful what you say. It is not so easy to do away with a witch. She can bring your house down to ruin around you. Too much harm has already been done."

VII

The rest of the day was a confusion of fatigue. Isabel burst into heartbroken tears when she saw her teacher, and had to be reassured and comforted and, finally, put to bed. *I might as well be the child's mother*, Daphne thought, looking at her innocent face as she dozed off. And was reminded, against her will, that if Miguel's suspicions were true it was her mother who had done this to her.

An ignorant old man, prejudiced against his employer's wife—of course his accusations were fantastic. But it was true that Pilar had not appeared to offer any help or consolation. She was in her own room as usual during the afternoon; no one knew what she did there, but Daphne could not imagine her reading or sewing or adding up the household accounts. It was hard to believe that she had actually brought Isabel into the world. There was no trace of the mother in the child, and Daphne was glad, even while she reproached herself for being uncharitable.

Finally she took her letter case into the garden, where Suzanne had arranged an old basket chair for her and a velvet hassock for her injured foot. Seated under a tree covered with big pink blossoms, whose name she didn't know, she found that she was too weary and too distrait to write letters. Anyway, what was there to say? The happenings of the last few weeks sounded more like episodes from a ghost story than the experiences of a sedate young governess.

The pain in her ankle had lessened, and she realized gratefully that even her short meeting with the lively little doctor had cheered her. Even matronly Mrs. Jackson, so like the good middle-aged women she had known at home, for all her accent was almost incomprehensible, was reassuringly ordinary. But a thread of unease ran through her thoughts, and finally, sitting with her letter paper in her lap, she realized what it was.

Charles had accepted Miguel's babble of witches and the evil eye quite matter-of-factly, as though the old man had been talking about the price of rice or the way to treat a spavined horse. Surely he didn't believe all that nonsense?

Of course, he was being kind to an ignorant old man. But she couldn't convince herself that that was his only reason. His expression and his harsh tone were all the proof she needed that he had in fact taken Miguel's accusations quite seriously.

Witchcraft! She looked around the garden, incredulously. It was relatively cool here, in the shade, and the afternoon air was rich with the perfume of summer flowers. It was the blossoming season for roses, azalea, cape jessamine and many flowers that were strange to her, most of them larger and showier than flowers at home. Insects chirped in the neglected grass. A bumblebee zoomed at her. She sat unmoving until he was gone.

In this world of light and color it was impossible to believe in the dark magic that Miguel talked about. But she remembered that in the night, when the air was like damp black velvet, she had been haunted by thoughts of the strange and supernatural. How many times had she peered out of her bedroom window with the uncanny feeling that something out there was watching her?

There was a slight sound behind her. She turned. Pilar stood there, holding a large tray. She looked proud and indifferent as always, but she said pleasantly enough, "I have brought your tea, since it's difficult for you to walk. I know that you like a cup in the afternoon, since you have not yet learned to drink our coffee."

"Oh, thank you, that's kind of you." And she was really touched by this unexpectedly friendly gesture on the part of one who had never paid her any special attention. She had to admit that the tray looked tempting, set with two fine bone china cups and a plate of Suzanne's ginger cookies.

Pilar said with a slight smile, "Charles made the tea. His mother liked it. Myself, I prefer our coffee, but it is difficult for strangers to accustom themselves to it." She bent over Daphne with the tray. "Please help yourself."

Shall I ask her to sit down? Daphne wondered. *After all, it's her garden. And what on earth am I going to talk to her about?* In her confusion, she overreached and found her hand above the farther cup. Still more embarrassing, her sleeve brushed against the cooky plate and almost knocked it off the tray. Pilar's eyes widened a little. *How can I be so clumsy?* Daphne thought. She took the cup her hand was touching and, to avoid conversation, tasted the tea. It was a little stronger than she liked it, but she reminded herself that bringing it had been an act of kindness.

She realized that Pilar's eyes were still fixed on her, and made a clumsy attempt to rise. "Won't you sit down? And you're not drinking your own tea."

"I don't care for it."

Then why carry it all the way from the kitchen? Daphne wondered. Pilar said smoothly, "Why don't you drink it, since your cup is almost empty? The sun is very hot—it will do you good."

"Perhaps, if you don't care for it."

"Of course. Have one of the little cookies. They're quite good."

The second cup of tea, now beginning to cool, was even stronger than the first. More, it had a strange bitter flavor, evident even through the lavish amount of sugar that had been poured into it. After the first sip she decided that she didn't really want it. She sat holding the cup in her hand, trying to find something to talk about and wishing that Pilar would go away.

"You are not drinking your tea."

"I'm sorry, I find that I don't want a second cup. It was kind of you to bring it, though. I feel like an idiot with this ankle—everyone has been so kind, and I'm making so much work for everyone."

Pilar's face closed and hardened. She snatched the cup from Daphne's hand and emptied it on the grass then piled the cups and saucers on the tray and walked away, graceful as ever but moving more rapidly than Daphne had ever seen her.

That wasn't very polite of her, the girl thought, feeling humiliated and a little guilty as well. It was the first friendly overture Pilar had ever made, and she had apparently, without meaning to committed some terrible blunder. Perhaps she should have forced the brew down, even though she didn't really want it. But it was too strong to be palatable—indeed, it was bitter as quinine. And all that sugar—

Her eyes widened.

Don't be silly, she told herself firmly. *It's all this stupid talk, and the little colt dying.*

Once, when she was about fourteen, she and half a dozen other schoolgirls had started telling grost stories. It was at Elsie Joy's, she remembered; the tales had started at the supper table, and by nine o'clock they were all afraid to go home in the dark. Elsie's father had taken them home by lantern light, and had teased them for a long time afterward. *If this keeps up I'll be seeing things every time I shut my eyes,* she thought, *just as we did that night.*

Charles made the tea.

Then why one cup with sugar? He knew that she never took it, and Pilar apparently did not drink tea at all. Or had she planned to, and then changed her mind?

I was meant to get that cup, Daphne reminded herself, stricken. *The bitter one was meant for me. She turned the tray around before she offered it, so that it would be on the right side. If I hadn't been clumsy and stupid, I'd have taken the sweetened cup.*

But Charles made the tea.

Then if something is wrong, they're both in it. He made it, and she brought it to me.

It was easy to believe that Pilar was a plotter of dark and evil deeds. But she could not accept Charles as a party to her wickedness.

Or was he really murderous, destructive? Did

Pilar moan and beg at night because she was afraid of him, not because he ignored her? Did he subject her to some torment that a stranger in the house could not know?

There was some antagonism between them that went deeper than the ordinary alienation of a married couple who had fallen out of love. She had sensed it at her first dinner in the dark old house, and had taken for granted that the root of the trouble lay in Pilar.

But if it were his behavior that was secretly hurtful, instead of hers?

I'm not safe here, she thought wildly. *Nobody is safe here, and Isabel least of all, the child of this oddly ill-assorted couple.* For a moment she had a wild vision of herself kidnapping Isabel and fleeing with her to the small snug world of Jordansville, Maine.

She shook her head. There was no earthly way to get Isabel away from her home and parents. And if the danger were real and not a figment of her over-exercised imagination, it was equally impossible to abandon her.

She decided it was high time to pull herself together. A series of odd coincidences, and she began telling herself ghost stories. *This is 1902,* she reminded herself. *Reasonable people don't believe in ghosts, or magic spells, or whatever it is that terrifies Miguel so.*

The thought of the little man was so strong that a few moments later, looking up to see him hobbling across the grass toward her, she thought for a second that she was imagining him. But he was carrying a slender dusty bottle and a thin glass, two objects outside the scope of her fancy. She welcomed him with a smile. He was a foreigner, a servant, an ignorant old man with his head crammed full of old-country superstitions, but she trused him.

"I bring you some of Don Jaime's sherry, *señorita*. Very gentle; very good for the body and soul, too. Will you drink it now?"

"Thank you, Miguel. Mrs. Osborne brought me some tea a few minutes ago." She wondered if she should tell him about the sweet-and-bitter cup, and reminded herself that she was making too much of a trivial incident. Besides, the old man already had enough odd ideas.

She went on nervously making polite talk. "Mr. Osborne made it. I suppose he used to make tea for his mother when she was alive, didn't he? Anyway, it was nice of him."

"*Señorita*."

His voice was low, almost a whisper, but it stopped her. "What's the matter?" It was all she could do to keep her voice calm. Her heart began to beat so hard that she could see the thin starched material of her shirtwaist rise and fall.

"He has been in the fields all afternoon, since he brought you back to the plantation. He has not even eaten his lunch."

A bee buzzed loudly in the sudden silence. Daphne looked around the garden before she spoke. "Then why did she say so? I didn't imagine it—I'm not making things up. She was the one who said that about his mother."

Miguel seemed not to hear. Dropping on one knee, he wrenched the cork out of the bottle's neck and let the pale golden liquid run into the thin glass. A new fragrance, delicate and light, was added to the mixed scents of the flowers. He offered her the glass. "Sip it slowly. The good wine was given by God for the use of men on this earth. I think you have need of it today." He looked at her sharply. "You may need it even more in the future."

The first sip was disappointingly flat. With the second, a gentle warmth began to spread through her. She lost a little of her tension. But the questions that troubled her were still unanswered. "Miguel, I'm afraid. Something is happening in this place, and I don't know what it is, but I am afraid of it."

"Are you afraid for yourself?"

"Most of all for Isabel. But I'm afraid for myself, too," she admitted.

"Do not trust that one, *señorita*. Do not trust her in anything. She has the evil eye."

"And what about him?" It was no surprise to her that he distrusted Pilar; she had known that from the first day. By this time it would have been no surprise to her to come upon Pilar mixing a witch's brew and muttering incantations. But to be forced to distrust Charles Osborne was more than she felt she could bear. If he were evil, who could be good?

Miguel said, "He has much trouble, but he is a good man. Never has he done any harm, not in his whole life."

He took the glass from her shaking hand and tipped a little more of the sunny wine into it. "She would cut her own child's throat to be revenged on one she hates, and her anger bursts into flame like a pine torch. Witches have no heart even for their young. They are children of the devil, and they have no heart."

VIII

The next three weeks were busy but uneventful. Daphne's ankle healed quickly. Looking around for a way to pass the time while she had to stay in the house, she remembered her scanty glimpses of the seldom-used downstairs rooms, and went through them again with Isabel tagging after her. The drawing room, sitting room and library were as richly furnished as the big dining room and in even worse condition, because they had been closed away so long. She wondered if it might be possible to clear away the dirt and cobwebs and let in the fresh air and sunshine.

Under any other circumstances she would have offered her services to the mistress of the plantation. With one elderly house servant to do the work of half a dozen, the average housewife would have been grateful for extra help, all the more since washing woodwork and beating carpets were not among the usual duties of a governess. But Pilar was far from being the average housewife. In fact, she was not a housewife at all. She didn't seem to notice how thickly the dust lay on the old chairs and tables, or how many of the fine thin porcelain plates and cups were chipped and cracked. Daphne could imagine the scornful curl of her lip if the governess were to ask her permission to clean and polish the furniture. She tried to put the project out of her mind.

But it kept coming back, and when she was finally able to walk without discomfort, she spoke to Suzanne about it. The housekeeper was delighted with her willingness to help and eager to be of assistance, even though she was already working from daybreak until late night. With Isabel's help, the two began one hot morning to refurbish the drawing room where Don Jaime and his Virginia-born bride had entertained the local aristocrats in the happy early years of their marriage.

It was a high, graciously proportioned room with French windows to the floor, shrouded in lace curtains that gave out billows of dust when Isabel shook them and wine-red velvet drapes with heavy tasseled gilt cords. The heavy paper that covered the walls was faded red and gold. "This wallpaper came all the way from Paris," Isabel said in awe, "around the Cape in a sailing vessel and then up the Mississippi from Orleans in a paddlewheel boat." She sighed happily. "The rug is from Persia—when are we going to get to Persia in our geography book, Miss Summerfield? They used to have dances here when Papa and Tio Felipe were little boys."

"They couldn't dance on a Persian rug."

"No, they put some kind of cloth down over

it." Isabel looked at Suzanne for confirmation. "There was a grand piano here, between the windows, and Antoine Frechette used to come over from Saint Jean Baptiste with his fiddle and play for the dancers. It must have been beautiful."

. She sounded as though she remembered it all. Daphne asked, amused, "Did your father tell you about it?"

"No, Tio Felipe did. Papa never used to tell me stories when I was small. He does now, sometimes. He is much nicer than he used to be."

Daphne had been rolling her sleeves well above the elbow while she listened. Now she wrung a piece of cheesecloth out of a bowl of hot water and shook it out, steaming. "First we'll wipe all the dust off the furniture with hot water," she explained, feeling that it was time to change the subject. "Then we rub in lemon oil until the wood shines. Can you do that?"

"I'll even polish the little tiny pictures." Isabel traced the grape and vine design that ran around an elaborately carved drum table. "My grandmother polished her own furniture. So did her mother in Virginia, and they had house slaves, but they took care of their heirlooms themselves. This will all be mine someday; Tio Felipe said so."

It was strange, but as the work advanced Daphne thought that she could understand the child's pride of ownership. It was no more unreasonable in a little girl who would be mistress of these rooms someday than in an outsider who would go away and never see Fairlawn again. It was as though the gracious furniture and heavily-framed paintings had belonged to her own ancestors, and she the one chosen to restore them to their oldtime beauty.

She knew that it was idiotic, less than a dream; it was a fantasy with no basis in fact. Her forebears had started out modestly enough with stoneware plates and tin pans from an itinerant peddler, hand-hemmed gingham curtains and patchwork quilts. But her delight in the fine grain and shine of rosewood, cherry and mahogany had a touch of the possessive in it, which she carefully hid from the chattering little girl and the silent woman who worked with her.

She reminded herself that no matter how short her stay was to be, she could enjoy bringing order and beauty where dirt and neglect had been. It was a creative act to sponge the antique rugs and see the soft rich reds and blues emerge, to take down the delicate lace curtains and help Suzanne wash them under the trees in the back yard and pin them carefully to the stretchers. They came out like dream cobwebs. The heavy velvet draperies split when they were brushed and shaken outdoors, but the three women hung them over freshly sparkling panes and arranged them to hide the cracks and threadbare spots.

"It doesn't show very much," Isabel reported, standing back and looking critically at the windows, "and anyhow, they don't make you sneeze now if you bump them."

Pilar, perhaps made curious by thumpings and footsteps in rooms that had long been closed, came in one day to see what they were doing. She stood in the doorway, her finely curved eyebrows raised inquiringly. Daphne said nervously, "Do you mind? It's such a beautiful room."

Pilar shrugged. "If it amuses you." Her voice was light, but an edge of contempt in it made Daphne feel both embarrassed and resentful. Pilar said, "There used to be a piano here. Felipe sold it." She walked away, like an adult leaving the children to their games.

Daphne picked up her sponge and went back to the picture frame she had been wiping, discovering with mingled amusement and fright that her knees were shaking.

Isabel said in her loud, clear childish voice, "Tio Felipe and my mama used to fight. I remember, before he and my papa went to Spain. Once she threw a platter at him."

Suzanne nodded, wide-eyed. Daphne said, "Let's think about something else, shall we? What shall we put in the spot where the piano used to be? The little desk with the mother-of-pearl panels?"

They had almost finished the "company" rooms when the rains began, unseasonable, not violent enough to ruin the crop, as Charles feared at first, but heavy enough to put a temporary stop to field work. Daphne and Isabel had done their lessons in the garden and on the shady lawn more often than in the second-floor classroom, breaking off for a walk or a canter around the pasture when Isabel became inattentive. Now they moved indoors. Isabel arranged her books, some of which the elder Osbornes had used as children, carried two coal-oil lamps up from the kitchen with proud care, and rummaged through the disused bedrooms until she found a chair to go with the battered table she used as a desk.

"My papa learned his lessons on this table," she said with a pleased sigh, "and Tio Felipe too. See, here are their initials." She added wistfully, "May I carve mine, too?"

Daphne hesitated. "Children are usually punished for carving furniture," she said finally, "but since your father's are there, why don't you ask him? After all, the table belongs to him."

Isabel nodded. "It's right nice in here when it's raining, don't you think so? May I read a story instead of studying my tables?"

"You may read a story *after* you do your tables," Daphne said primly. Catching a glimpse of the tall figure in the doorway, she suppressed the smile that always came to the surface when Isabel came up with one of her ideas. "Write the eights and nines for me, please, in your best penmanship."

"Yes, Miss Summerfield. Oh, Papa!" Isabel jumped up and wrapped herself around her father. "Can I put my initials on the school table, like you and Tio Felipe?"

Over her head, Osborne's eyes met Daphne's. The effect was rather like that of mild electric shock. "I should think so, if you keep them very small. You understand that people don't use knives on the furniture as a regular thing."

Isabel said with great dignity, "I know all about furniture. Miss Summerfield and I rubbed everything in the drawing room with beeswax and lemon oil." She added honestly, "Suzanne did a lot, too."

"Oh, so you two are responsible for all the fixing up? Isn't that pretty heavy work after a day with a lively child?"

Daphne blushed slightly. "It's beautiful furniture—I enjoyed working with it. Suzanne has enough to do." It occurred to her, too late, that he might take that as a criticism of Pilar and the way the house was managed, or left to manage itself. She looked away.

Charles said slowly, "My mother had those tables and cabinets brought from her girlhood home in Virginia, after her mother died and the land was sold. Fairlawn, the plantation her family had there. My stepfather had this house built and the grounds laid out from the plan of the original Fairlawn, hoping it would reconcile her to living in Louisiana." He shook his head. "There has been too much sorrow here, beginning with my mother's death and then Don Jaime's, less than a year later. Perhaps I can bring the good times back for Isabel and her children."

"I'm sure you will."

He detached Isabel's arms from around his neck. "Here, kitten, take my pocket knife and put your name where you like. Small letters, you understand? And don't cut yourself."

"I'll put it between you and Tio Felipe." Her sunny head bent over the table. "I miss Tio Felipe, Papa. I dream about him sometimes."

A series of expressions crossed Charles' face:

pleasure, sorrow, caution. He made no answer, but turned to Daphne. "I owe you a double debt, Miss Summerfield, for my daughter's upbringing and for my mother's treasured furniture."

She said demurely, "Isabel is an excellent student, and I enjoy working with beautiful chairs and tables."

"I can't tell you how I felt when I looked into the large drawing room and saw everything as it was in my parents' time."

"'Cept the piano," Isabel reminded him.

"Yes. Well, I had to sell that to pay the taxes. Otherwise we might have lost Fairlawn. No help for it."

Isabel looked at him with big eyes. "Why, Papa, it was Tio Felipe who sold the piano!"

There was a silence. Charles said, "We both agreed on it. Come on, kitten, aren't you supposed to be writing your tables? You're wasting a lot of time, it seems to me."

The atmosphere in the room had changed completely. Daphne went to her desk and sat down, opening the first book her hand fell upon. "Won't you have a chair, Mr. Osborne?"

"Thanks, but I'm helping Miguel mend harness."

The rain, which only a few minutes before had seemed to enclose the schoolroom in a cozy little world of its own, sounded dreary as it beat against the gray windowpanes. Daphne felt suddenly tired. Her gaze fell on her hands, nicely shaped but still red and rough from the hours of scrubbing and polishing they had accomplished. Like a servant's hands. *Well*, she thought defensively, *honest work is nothing to be ashamed of.*

Charles, at the door, turned back. "We'll be able to use the drawing room tomorrow evening," he said pleasantly enough. "I'm driving to Saint Laurent in the afternoon to meet a buyer from Whitney, Hildebrand and Leroux—commission brokers," he explained in answer to Daphne's questioning look. "You girls put on your best bibs and tuckers. We don't often have a guest for dinner, and this one is an important man in our future. If he likes us, he may buy our rice."

Daphne protested, "You don't want me to come to dinner if you're having a guest."

"Certainly I do. What would you do, have a bowl of cold grits in the kitchen? Besides, someone has to keep an eye on this child's table manners."

Isabel still sulking over being sent back to her lessons gave him a resentful look over her penholder. Daphne secretly sympathized with her. Whatever gaps there might be in her formal education, Isabel's social behavior would have done credit to many a grown-up, and she had a pleasant ease that a social bud might have envied.

Charles ignored the look. "Besides," he said with a twinkle, "I invited Mr. Whitney especially for you. He's a bachelor. Highly eligible, too."

"Mr. Osborne—"

The door closed quietly behind him.

Daphne sat looking at the blurry window, forgetting to watch what Isabel was doing. Her heart was thumping with terrified anticipation.

IX

All the next day her mind was filled with the age-old feminine question of what to wear. Since her wardrobe was decidedly modest, she had been glad to discover upon her arrival at Fairlawn that none of the Osborne's made any attempt to dress for special occasions. In fact, they seemed not to have any special occasions. Charles bathed before dinner and put on fresh work clothes no less shabby than those he had worn all day, but washed and ironed by Suzanne's devoted hands. Daphne, like her pupil, was content to smooth her hair and perhaps put on a fresh blouse in the evening. In fact, Isabel would gladly have lived in riding clothes.

As for Pilar, she seemed to have an endless supply of ruffled silks and muslins, all of them more elaborate than Daphne thought suitable for the mother of a ten-year-old child but very well suited to her erect figure, slender yet deep-bosomed, and she wore them without regard to what she was doing at the moment. Her hair was as black and smooth as a crow's wing and she wore it pulled severely back from her clear-cut face, in a chignon at the nape of her neck; sometimes she thrust a flower or a jeweled pin into the knot, which looked as solid and unyielding as ebony. Like the frivolous slippers which set off her high arches, Pilar's clothes were selected with no regard for either style or suitability, but as an expression of her own exotic personality.

Daphne could hardly imagine her in a tailored suit and shirtwaist, or a gingham apron.

She was a little shaken when Pilar came into the schoolroom a few minutes after Charles' departure with a mass of ruffles and flounces over her arm. "Miss Summerfield, can you mend? Suzanne is so wrapped up in preparations for this stupid dinner, it's useless to ask her for help."

It was on the tip of the girl's tongue to remind her that Suzanne was doing the work of three or four people, even without the added demands of a company dinner. She suppressed the words. "What needs to be done?"

"Some of the ruffles were torn the last time I wore this dress." Pilar's face took on the sullen look it often wore when she was faced with a practical problem. "We never go anywhere; we have no need for evening dress. Charles is being stubborn as usual."

It was Daphne's first intimation that formal wear would be called for. Her heart sank as she examined the damaged ruffles. The dress was pale yellow, of a heavy satin that draped beautifully but would be uncomfortably hot in that almost tropical climate. It was an easy matter to take the few necessary stitches, smoothing the flounces so that the repairs didn't show. Daphne wondered, holding it up for a last inspection, whether she too would be expected to honor the occasion with a kind of dress she had never owned or expected to own.

Her fears were justified when Pilar retired to try on the yellow satin and came back for a last inspection. The bodice was cut far lower than

71

anything she had ever seen, except in historical paintings. Pilar's beautiful neck and shoulders rose from it as smooth as ivory. The silk material hugged her waist and bosom, and widened gradually into an elaborate arrangement of lace-edged ruffles, forming a small train in the back. She had put on small matching slippers with bows, and a high jeweled comb topped her coiffure.

Daphne thought that her attire was more suitable for a state reception than a quiet dinner at home, but there was no way she could express this opinion. Nor did her disapproval solve her own problem. She was glad when Pilar gathered up her little train and left without bothering to say thank you. The elaborate costume seemed to widen the gulf between them, never yet crossed.

Now, the following day, Isabel was still thinking about the yellow dress. She closed her book with a happy sigh. "Don't you think my mother will look beautiful tonight? What are you going to wear, Miss Summerfield?"

Daphne tried to smile. "I think I'd better have something in the kitchen, Isabel. I haven't anything except my Sunday dress."

Isabel's forehead puckered. "I'm going to wear my white organdy with the silk sash Tio Felipe sent me from Spain. But you're a grown-up lady. You must have a beautiful silk dress that leaves your arms bare."

"Unfortunately, dear, there's no way to get one between now and dinner time. Even if I had the material, it would be impossible to make anything in time."

"If I were a fairy godmother, like the one who made Cinderella's coach out of a pumpkin, I'd turn your Sunday dress into a beautiful gown all covered with diamonds." Isabel's eyes widened. "Miss Summerfield, why don't you wear one of *Mamacita's* dresses? There's a whole closet full of them. I don't think anyone would mind."

"Your grandmother's dresses? I couldn't do that. Besides, they wouldn't fit me."

"Yes, they would. Have you ever seen her picture in the big bedroom? She was little, like you, and her hair was golden and curly. When I look at you I can almost remember her. Not really," she added with her usual careful honesty, "because she died when I was a baby, but sometimes I think I can."

Daphne struggled with temptation. She didn't have to take the pink muslin Sunday dress out of her wardrobe to know that it wouldn't do. Next to Pilar's elaborately ruffled satin, the high collar, innocent puffed sleeves and little ribbon sash she had chosen for Sunday morning services in the village church became pathetic and insignificant. But there was nothing else.

Nor was there any way she could stay away from the dinner table, even on pretense of illness. Charles would be upset and hurt by her refusal. He might even be capable of lifting her out of bed and carrying her to the table in her nightgown. The sprained ankle episode had shown her what determination lay under his habitual gentle courtesy; it also explained a great

73

many things that she had wondered about, why Isabel was as well brought up as she was, why Pilar's discontent seldom went beyond silent sulking. He was a masterful man.

Without having convinced herself that she had any right to do so, after lunch she let Isabel lead her to the big square corner bedroom at the head of the stairs. She looked around curiously. In her attempts to clean and order the old rooms, she had not opened the door of the room where Jaime and Camilla Ramirez had slept all the years of their married life. The wide four-poster was covered with an elaborate lace spread, and Camilla's silver brushes and mirrors were arranged as she had left them on the dressing table. She glanced around cautiously, as though the mistress of the room might walk in at any moment. "Isabel, I really don't think—"

"There she is, my papa's mother."

The painting was dimmed by time and neglect, but she could see that Charles Osborne's mother had indeed been beautiful. Petite and poised, with her crown of golden-brown curls held proudly, she looked out of the golden frame with deep blue eyes as direct as Isabel's. Although the child was tall, like her father, Daphne realized that she had inherited her forthright and loving nature as well as her coloring from her grandmother. Now for the first time, she was thankful to find so little of the child's own mother in her.

Isabel, practical as ever, wasted no time. Reverently but eagerly, she opened the doors of the vast carved armoire that dominated one wall. A scent of faded flowers flowed into the room, the ghost of a perfume. Daphne had a confused impression of bright and delicate colors, laces, flounces, embroidery, full swinging skirts. In spite of her qualms, she began to feel the sweet excitement of a woman in a dress shop. She asked doubtfully, "Do you really think it would be all right?"

"Here's a pink one with silver lace. You'd look beautiful in it."

"Too elaborate." She didn't intend to say so, lest she sound critical of Pilar, but she privately thought that the gown was cut much too low. It was all very well for Pilar, brought up in a different kind of life, to display her neck and arms. The very thought of appearing in deep décolletage made her blush hotly. *Perhaps,* she thought, *you have to be an aristocrat not to mind. Or a gypsy.*

She began to sort out the confusion of colors and materials, partly to keep Isabel from pulling everything out and partly because she was beginning to wonder whether she might, after all, borrow one of these beautiful silk gowns. None of them could have been more than ten or twelve years old, not long enough to make them passé in a part of the country where fashion inclined more to frills than elegance.

Isabel said hopefully, "How about this one?"

It was a light but intense blue, the color of cornflowers in the sunshine, and it was simply made of a thin, crisp silk with skirt panels of pastel embroidery. The neck was rounded, not too low, and the little puffed sleeves were covered with the same embroidery. It was the dress of her dreams, the dress she would have chosen if all the lovely dresses in the world had been displayed before her dazzled eyes.

Isabel said, as though she had been the adult and Daphne a school-age daughter, "Why don't you try it on? If it doesn't fit, we'll have to find another one."

Daphne's heart thumped as she closed the door of the room, touched a match to each of the dusty candles on the bureau, and removed her practical skirt and shirtwaist. The blue silk made a whispering sound as it slid over her head. It was a trifle snug around the waist, but perfect otherwise. Only the tip of her last summer's slippers would show under the full skirt. For a moment she wished that she had a pair of high-heeled shoes such as Pilar habitually wore, but she put it out of her mind. No use dreaming of the impossible.

"You're beautiful, Miss Summerfield. Just as beautiful as my *Mamacita*."

She took the pins out of her hair, brushed it and piled it high, coaxing the little tendrils that framed her face into soft curls. Jewels? A string of pearls would be right, but she might as well wish for the rainbow. She would wear the little heart-shaped locket that had been her mother's only ornament and was now her chief treasure.

Candle in hand, she looked into the big mirror.

A beautiful young woman in flower-embroidered silk looked back at her. Golden brown hair piled high, violet-blue eyes in a heart-shaped

76

face. She smiled, and dimples showed at the corners of her mouth.

I may not be beautiful, she thought, taking off the blue dress and laying it carefully across a chair, *but I'm not ugly.* Her heart sang as she got into her everyday clothes and ran down the back stairs to see if Suzanne needed any help in the kitchen.

The kitchen was full of wonderful odors, the tables covered with platters and trays. Miguel had brought from somewhere big chunks of greenish-white ice for the wooden chest on the back porch. Daphne followed Suzanne as she set a bowl of something pink and foamy to chill. Other delicacies were already in the chest, a bowl of small pink shrimps, colored jellies topped with swirls of whipped cream, chicken salad with the rich dressing Suzanne mixed drop by drop, tasting and measuring with religious care.

"It's beautiful, Suzanne. Everything looks wonderful."

There was even a cake with blanched almonds set in patterns on the thick creamy icing. Plainly, Suzanne had everything well in hand. Satisfied, Daphne asked, "What time is dinner?" Suzanne held up seven fingers, beaming with pride in her own culinary achievements.

By six she had given Isabel a last-minute inspection, tied the brocaded sash from Spain and brushed the child's curls into perfect cylinders. Isabel went to the veranda to watch for her father and the guest, not sitting on the steps as usual but settling herself in ladylike primness on a hassock. Daphne was free to ornament herself as best she could.

She lighted all the candles in her bedroom: two on the washstand, two on the bureau and one on her bedside table. The image in the pier glass almost took her breath away. A slender stranger in blue silk that fell softly to the floor, her crown of golden curls shining, violet eyes lighted from within by excitement. She fastened the golden locket around her neck and descended the stairs slowly, holding her skirts up with instinctive grace.

Charles and Mr. Whitney had not arrived. Pilar was in her own room, doing whatever it was that occupied so much of her time. Daphne went into the drawing room and sat down on the brocade sofa, with a leather-bound volume from the library open on her lap. Tonight, as never before, she felt herself a part of Fairlawn—a part of the colorful and romantic life of the old days, before loss and poverty darkened the destiny of the plantation.

She was not sure how much time passed before there was a flurry at the front door, the counterpoint of two male voices and Isabel's delighted laugh ringing out. Footsteps echoed down the long hall and stopped at the drawing room door. She looked up, smiling.

Charles Osborne stood in the doorway, tall and impressive in his formal black and satin tie. Isabel and a stranger were directly behind him, but Daphne saw them as blurs. Her gaze was riveted to Charles' face. He had gone ashen-white at the sight of her, and he reached for the doorjamb as though he were dizzy.

He said in a hoarse voice, "Good God—*Madre-cita!*"

X

Pilar's voice cut sharply into the silence. "What is going on here?"

She moved into the candlelit drawing room, the two men mechanically standing aside to let her pass. She was a beautiful and impressive figure in her satin gown, her dark eyes boring into Daphne's face. Instinctively, the girl half-closed her eyes to avoid that accusing look.

"Where did you get that dress? How dare you wear it here!"

Isabel stepped forward and threw her arms around Daphne. "I took it from *Mamacita's* wardrobe. Doesn't she look beautiful?"

The color came back into Charles' face. He put an arm around his daughter's shoulders, so that, for a moment, the three of them made an intertwined group with Pilar and the young man looking on. Daphne, smiling shakily, moved away. "I'm sorry. I'll retire at once."

"Nonsense, you look very nice. You must forgive my surprise. You do look very much like my mother—so much so that for a moment I thought I was seeing a ghost! The dress is most becoming. I'm glad that you found it and decided to wear it."

79

Pilar flushed, but the presence of a guest prevented her from saying anything more. Charles went on smoothly, apparently recovered from his initial shock. "Pilar, may I present Mr. Whitney? Miss Summerfield, Mr. Whitney. Miss Summerfield is a valued member of our household. You've already met my daughter."

Mr. Whitney bowed over Pilar's gracefully extended hand, then took Daphne's and held it, she felt, a little longer than was necessary. He was a rather stocky but well-built young man with wavy dark hair and large brown eyes, much better dressed than his host but not nearly as handsome, Daphne thought. "It's a great pleasure to meet three such charming young ladies." Tactfully he smiled at Isabel, who beamed back at him.

Suzanne appeared before an embarrassing silence could set in, smiling beneath the snowy cap that had replaced her tignon. Charles said easily, "I believe that dinner is ready. Shall we adjourn to the dining room?"

He had regained his self-possession, but he was pale and the lines of strain at his mouth and eyes were deeper than she had ever seen them. She watched him anxiously as he seated Pilar at the long table and then turned his attention to the bottle of wine Suzanne was offering for his consideration. "We live very simply, Mr. Whitney. I trust you will be comfortable, however."

"You have a beautiful house." Davis Whitney looked around the dining room. The heavy old furniture glowed softly in the candlelight, and the threadbare areas in the rug and curtains were not noticeable as they would have been by daylight. Daphne noticed that Suzanne had found five place settings without cracks and mars, and the tablecloth, which the housekeeper had spent several hours ironing, fell to the floor in glossy splendor. Whitney said pleasantly, "You've kept all the charm of the Old South. My people lost their home in the War Between the States—my father started his brokerage firm in the back room of an uncle's drygoods store."

Daphne felt herself warm to him. This was something she could understand, even though her own grandfather had fought on the other side of the bloody conflict and had fallen at Gettysburg. Charles said, "He has much to be proud of. Your firm is one of the most respected in the South."

"Thanks to forward-looking growers like yourself, sir. But the ladies are finding all this talk of business dull. May I compliment you on your cook, ma'am?"

"Thank you." Pilar's tone was indifferent. Isabel glanced at her mother, then bent over the soup plate Suzanne had just placed in front of her. Daphne wished uneasily that she were sitting closer to the little girl, to give her a warning look or touch if she began to explain the domestic situation. She knew how much work and planning Suzanne had put into this dinner; a tactless word from the child would have spoiled the impression the old servant was trying to make on her employer's account. But Isabel was on her best behavior. She seemed at her ease among all

the heavy spoons and forks, and remained silent
unless one of the grown-ups spoke to her.

Perhaps, Daphne thought, Isabel took her way
of living for granted because she had never
known any other.

She herself felt much less self-assured than
her pupil. She was acutely conscious of her borrowed dress and the stir it had caused. Even
though she had hesitated to wear it, had over-
come some moral scruples in order to do so, she
knew that the gown both fitted and became her.
And she could not have predicted any of the
varied reactions the other three were showing:
Charles' shock, the cold disapproval in Pilar's
eyes, or the frank admiration on the young
guest's face whenever he looked at her.

If her appearance had upset her employer, it
was more than acceptable to Mr. Whitney. He
listened to Charles' table talk and made polite
replies; with five diners at one end of the great
table, there was no chance for anyone to start a
private conversation. But she was aware of his
admiring glances and the flattering tone of his
voice when he addressed a remark to her.

The soup plates cleared away, Suzanne
brought on a bewildering assortment of foods,
some of which Daphne was unable to recognize.
She helped herself politely, admiring anew Suzanne's skill and patience which made it possible
for her to take over the duties of an entire domestic staff. Not for the first time, she wondered why
none of the local people worked at Fairlawn.
Wages were low hereabouts, so the Osbornes'
straitened circumstances were surely not the

only reason. As often before, she decided that Suzanne, being from Virginia, was probably unwilling to have the local people in her kitchen. Or perhaps they distrusted her, both because she was "foreign" and because her inability to speak set her apart.

Or was it possible that the eerie happenings at Fairlawn had become known through the countryside? That would explain not only the isolation of Suzanne and Miguel, but the way their master and mistress lived. The aura of mystery that hung over the run-down plantation, added to the belief of the ignorant in "haunts" and spells, would be enough to keep them away.

Davis Whitney's questioning look brought her out of her revery. She smiled at him and ventured to taste her wine, which was cool on her tongue but sent little waves of warmth through her.

Pilar said sharply, startled out of her usual calm, "Carlos, are you eating shrimp? But it makes you ill, always."

Charles gave her a look of utter amazement. Then his face changed. He said calmly, "I seem to be all over that. Anyway, let's not be concerned about it. These little Gulf shrimp are worth a few blotches and itches."

"A few? *Dios*, have you forgotten how you suffered the last time, and the family with you?" She scowled darkly. "Husbands are difficult. No doubt your wife finds you so, Mr. Whitney?"

"She probably will when I'm fortunate enough to find one," Whitney said cheerfully. "I have a clear picture of my dream lady, as I suppose most young men have, but there is no assurance that she'll care about me if I ever find her. However, I can enjoy shrimps in perfect safety, so she need have no anxiety on that account."

"And what is your dream lady like?"

"Like Orlando's, just as high as my heart, with little golden curls around her forehead and a dimple in each cheek."

Isabel said, "That's how Miss Summerfield looks."

Charles said, "Isabel, eat your dinner." He, too, looked at Daphne. She had a feeling that he had never really seen her before; at any rate, she had never seen just that expression on his face. Pilar's eyes followed those of the two men, but it was not admiration that showed on her clear features. For a moment, Daphne had a glimpse of naked hate. Then it vanished, and the beautiful ivory face was passive, a little bored.

Charles said, "You know, Whitney, Miss Summerfield does resemble my mother. It's not only the dress, but the shape of her face and something in her expression. Forgive me for being personal, Miss Summerfield."

"It's quite all right." But she was unable to look at either of the men.

Isabel said eagerly, "My grandfather fell in love with my grandmother at first sight, and so did Don Jaime when he met her on a visit to his cousins in Tidewater. She was the belle of the county, even after she was a widow."

"Isabel."

Davis Whitney said gallantly, "I can quite understand that." But his look made the remark a compliment to Daphne.

The dinner moved on slowly, course after course of delicious food served in leisurely manner with the appropriate wines, and punctuated by talk about gardening, local happenings, and the plays Mr. Whitney had recently seen. "Perhaps you were brought up to believe that theatergoing is wicked, Miss Summerfield? One of my cousins married a Massachusetts man, and I became acquainted with that rather melancholy viewpoint when she brought him to visit us. We must make up a theater party next winter—you must all come to New Orleans as guests of my parents. The ladies will enjoy shopping. My mother's cousin Vivienne Chamfort says that New Orleans is second only to Paris in the elegance of its shops."

Daphne wondered what she would use for money if the trip ever materialized. Indeed, how could Charles afford it? The well-served food and the faded splendor of the house, looking its best in the dim light, had apparently given the guest a false picture of the Osborne family fortunes. Daphne realized with a slight feeling of guilt that her own position in the household had been left vague, whether deliberately or through an oversight she did not know. Perhaps Whitney thought she was a relative of Charles'.

She said gently, less to make her excuses than to explain her situation, "It might be rather difficult to get away. I am Isabel's governess and companion, you know."

"That must be interesting."

She did not know whether she had hoped or feared that his smiling admiration would be lessened if he knew she was an outsider here. As far as she could tell, it made no difference. He closed the subject by turning to Pilar. "Your cook is not a Creole, is she?"

"No, Carlos' mother brought her from Virginia."

Cook and housekeeper and entire staff, Daphne thought. When the seemingly endless meal finally came to a close with bitter coffee served in the drawing room, she murmured an excuse and slipped back to the kitchen, curious to know how Suzanne was managing. She realized, as the door of the drawing room closed behind her, that she also wanted to get away from the others for a few minutes. She was having more than her share of attention, and it was disturbing.

She opened the kitchen door and looked in.

Miguel was standing at the large kitchen table wiping dishes, an apron tied around his middle. Stacks of plates were piled around him. Turning, he frowned. Then he saw who it was and a smile creased his leathery face. "*Buenas noches, señorita.* How beautiful you are this evening. The Doña Camilla would have been pleased to see you in that fine blue dress.

"I came to see if you need any help."

"No, no, all goes well. Look, Suzanne, how beautiful she is. Like the Doña Camilla with her golden hair and the big eyes no?"

It had not been all Charles' imagination, then. Daphne smiled uneasily and went back to the drawing room, where a lazy and rather sleepy conversation had gotten under way. She felt empty and tired, after so much excitement. Sitting in a low chair, her hands folded in her lap, she tried to follow the talk. But her eyelids kept drooping.

She had not realized that Davis Whitney would be spending the night. She felt both troubled and relieved when Charles announced, "The corner room has been prepared for you, Mr. Whitney. I will show you there when you are ready to retire. Isabel, it's long past your bedtime. Perhaps Miss Summerfield will hear your prayers and tuck you in."

"Oh, Papa."

Davis Whitney said pleasantly, "It's past my bedtime, too, Miss Isabel. I won't cry if you won't." Isabel giggled. He turned to Pilar. "A delicious dinner, Mrs. Osborne, and I thank you for a delightful evening."

Pilar's voice was indifferent. "Thank you, Mr. Whitney. Suzanne will bring your breakfast whenever you ring for it. Good night." And as an afterthought, "Good night, Isabel. Miss Summerfield."

As though we were all servants and the house belonged to her, Daphne thought. And was chilled to remember that, after all, it did. She was Don Jaime's natural heir, as Charles was his legal one. Each had a firm claim.

She reminded herself that it hardly concerned her. But she resented anything that could diminish him as master of these acres and this house.

In her own room, she disrobed carefully and

laid the blue dress across the back of the slipper chair, planning to return it to Doña Camilla's closet in the morning. It had been a tiring evening. Partly exciting and partly scary, she decided. She was glad that it was over.

Davis Whitney's regard was a little alarming —or was that only because of the circumstances of their meeting? She had not been without beaux at home, but this poised young man made her uneasy. She decided, settling down in bed and tucking in the mosquito net, that she was imagining things. He was a handsome, well-mannered young man, and his behavior was perfectly courteous. But she wished that his eyes didn't light up when he looked at her. She didn't want to be looked at like that.

She fell asleep thinking about the unreasonableness of women, herself included. They were piqued when men ignored them and resentful when men admired them.

Much later, she was half-aroused by footsteps in the hall. They came to a stop at her door. She lay still for a moment, listening. There was no sound. *I was dreaming,* she decided. She turned over and went to sleep.

XI

It was late. The little traveling clock on her bedside table said nine-thirty, and a splinter of sunlight lay across the carpet, but the house was quiet. She found her slippers, got out of bed and pulled open the heavy curtains.

A flood of sunshine poured into the room, lying in golden waves on the floor and picking out the carving of the ornate furniture. Daphne wonderedly idly whether Isabel had had her breakfast, and then, as the memory of the previous evening's dinner party came flooding back, whether Davis Whitney had gone somewhere with Charles or was making himself at home downstairs, waiting to be entertained. She hoped that he was out and away; she needed time to regain her composure.

Thinking of him reminded her of Doña Camilla's blue dress. She must examine it carefully before putting it away. She crossed the room, reached to take it from the chair—and stopped, aghast.

The dress had been slashed to ribbons. She picked it up, and long strips of material fell to the floor.

The room darkened and whirled around her. She grasped the back of the chair and stood fighting for consciousness, until things righted themselves and she could breathe freely again.

Who had done such a thing? How, without her knowledge? And why? Why would anyone destroy a beautiful and harmless thing, a few yards of fine silk and with no life of its own?

There was no lock on her door. Anyone could have entered the room while she was asleep; tired as she was when she went to bed, she could have slept through anything. Someone had crept in on silent feet, carrying a knife or scissors, to wreck and destroy.

Charles, moved to a belated anger because she had profaned the memory of his mother—the necessity for public courtesy over? Or Pilar, for some strange reason of her own? Pilar had asked no questions after her first outcry, had behaved with her habitual courteous indifference. But Daphne was never sure what lay behind that unrevealing façade.

Shivering, she gathered up the fragments of material and rolled them together, then threw the little bundle into the back of her closet. She would find a way to dispose of it later. Or Suzanne would.

No. She could not share this frightening secret with anyone, because there was no way to know who was her enemy in this house, who was trying to destroy her. To admit fear might be to play into the hands of an unidentified foe.

Why the dress? For the first time, it crossed her mind that the midnight intruder could have destroyed her as easily as a harmless length of silk and embroidery. A sharp knife, a large pair of shears—she shuddered, seeing herself bound and gagged and helpless. *I must get out of this place*, she thought in panic.

Danger lay around her like a scent on the air, a whisper on the wind. Secret, intangible, invisible, not to be evaded because she did not know from which direction it came.

She managed to dress in spite of her shaking hands, combed and pinned up her hair, washed her face in lukewarm water from the Sèvres pitcher. Tense, she opened the bedroom door and peered out into the hall. It was empty as usual. For the first time she realized how silent this house was, except for Isabel's chatter.

She decided reasonably that she would have some breakfast before taking any other step. The thought of Suzanne's cheerful smile and tidy kitchen restored her courage. For all her dark-brown skin and eternal silence, Suzanne belonged to the world of familiar and trusted things. Feeling better, she went quietly down the wide stairs, sunlit from the window on the landing, and pushed open the door of the little breakfast room.

Charles and Davis Whitney were sitting at the table, drinking coffee and talking.

She had not expected them so late in the day. For a moment she was unable to speak or move. The men got hastily to their feet, Charles breaking off in mid-sentence. Whitney smiled confidently at her. She said quickly, "Please don't let me disturb you. I want to see Suzanne."

"Sit down," Charles said, in the same tone he used to Isabel. "I'll fetch your breakfast." She came around the table and pulled out a chair for her. She sat down, still upset but feeling happier and safer at the sound of his voice. He vanished into the kitchen.

Davis Whitney turned his flashing smile on her. "Miss Summerfield, you look charming this morning. Last night I'd have said that blue was your color, but that pink blouse is most becoming."

Her smile was tremulous. She wondered if it

were a Southern custom to notice ladies' clothing. The young men she had known at home would have thought it beneath them. Then the realization of what had happened to the blue dress shook her. Whitney went on, pleasantly making small talk, "We were up at daybreak. I'm pleased to find that Charles has adopted the Creole custom of a small black in the middle of the morning. My mother was a Beaumarchais, and I must admit that I like the old ways."

"Miss Summerfield is a tea drinker," Charles said, returning from the kitchen with a cup and saucer in one hand and a laden plate in the other. "I took the liberty of bringing you some ham and eggs as well, since I know that you don't care for grits. You'll need a solid beginning to the day if we are to go to the island. It's a long trip, going and returning."

The delicate fragrance of the tea carried her back to that day in the garden, when she had taken the wrong cup. Pilar said that Charles made the strange-tasting tea. Miguel denied it. Who was lying? The shock and terror of that afternoon came back in full force, so that for a moment she was unable to speak. At last, conscious that both men were looking at her questioningly, she asked, "Did—did you make the tea?"

"Suzanne did, so you needn't be afraid of it."

How had he guessed? He went on cheerfully, "However, I can do a few simple things in the kitchen, so you needn't be so scornful!" His eyes twinkled.

Thank goodness, he had not guessed her doubts. He thought she was dubious about his ability to brew a cup of tea! She picked up the cup, trying to control the shaking of her hand.

Miguel was right. This was a man who could be hurt, but not one to hurt others.

She relaxed a little. The food was delicious, and she had learned that this sultry, languid climate called for hot foods, unreasonable as that seemed. She could appreciate the reviving effect of the "small blacks" that not only Pilar but Suzanne and Miguel took several times a day, even though she had not learned to drink the chicory-flavored coffee without cream or sugar. She sipped the thin delicious tea slowly. Face to face with Charles across a sunny table, a low bowl of single yellow roses perfuming the air, it was incredible that she had ever doubted him. And the frank admiration in young Mr. Whitney's eyes, which had embarrassed her last night, was reassuring this morning.

At least, she thought, the borrowed dress was not the only thing that had attracted him to her the night before. In her gray cotton skirt and simple pink gingham shirtwaist, her hair coiled around her head, she could still bring to his face the look of a boy admiring a pretty girl. She wondered suddenly why she thought of him as a boy. He was a trusted partner in his father's thriving grain brokerage business, he could not have been more than four or five years younger than Charles. But of course, marriage and parenthood brought maturity to men as well as women.

Reminded of her duties, she asked, "Where is Isabel?"

"Excused from lessons for today," Charles informed her, "and helping Suzanne pack the picnic baskets. Apparently we can't have a picnic without several kinds of food. We children used to spend whole days on Hidden Island with no more than a cold biscuit and a piece of ham stolen from the kitchen, but my daughter is a young lady. She has grown-up ideas at the age of ten."

"You were boys," Daphne reminded him with spirit.

"Pilar wasn't! But she could run faster and swim better than we could—and fight as well, too. She was a wildcat," Charles laughed, "and she didn't mind biting and scratching if she was getting the worst of it."

Whitney said, "But the bayous can be dangerous."

"For those who don't know them, yes. There are alligators, cottonmouths, moccasins and plenty of quicksands. Smugglers, too, in the old days. The Negroes believe the swamps are full of haunts. But to us, the bayous were like our back yard. We came and went like the Cajuns, who are more at home in a boat than on dry land."

Davis Whitney said, "Don't be alarmed, Miss Summerfield. We'll keep the snakes and crocodiles away, and the smugglers, too. I've never seen a haunt, though my great-aunts believe in them. Perhaps we ought to take along a sprinkle of uncrossing powder, just in case."

Not there, Daphne thought with sudden sharpness. Here at Fairlawn, where strange things prowled in the night and there was a malign influence in the air, a hate that did harm. She wondered how it was that Fairlawn, built because of a man's love for his beautiful wife, should fall prey to evil influences.

Don't be silly, she reminded herself. *There are no ghosts or spirits. If harm is done, it's done by living people.*

She realized that Charles was watching her closely. She put down her cup and pushed back her chair. "Perhaps I can help Suzanne, too. There must be a great deal to do."

"Oh, I'm sure she and Isabel have everything in order. They are old hands at this. We'll be ready to leave in half an hour."

Whitney said, "Just time for Miss Summerfield to show me the gardens. It's a beautiful day, and I have already heard of the Ramirez roses."

Try as she might, she could think of no reason for refusing. She said, "Of course, I'll be glad to."

At least, she thought as they walked through the echoing hall and into the sunshine-flooded outdoors, *I'll be out of this house for a few hours.* The shadowy house with secrets lurking in the corners, as airy as cobwebs and far harder to destroy.

XII

It was a long time since she had been on a picnic. The word had a cheerful homelike ring to it: it brought back memories of Sundays at the

state park, with a dozen or so young people singing as they jounced over the country roads in a
farm wagon; beach lunches, the girls giggling as
they held up their skirts and waded into the surf;
sleighrides, with everyone tucked away in a cozy
layer of hay and a boy's mittened hand holding
hers.

The thought of snow made her more than ever
conscious of the oppressive heat. She glanced at
Pilar, who seemed superior to weather of any
kind. She was sitting erect on the front seat of
the buggy, ignoring Charles, at her side, but now
and then addressing a remark to the three in
back. Daphne wondered why her employ-
er's wife had come along on this outing, whether
she saw it as an obligation of hospitality or was
trying to please her husband. That, too, was unlikely. She seemed as little interested in him as
in the rest of the party.

In the face of her indifference, Daphne could
hardly believe that this cold-faced woman was
a midnight accuser, a creature who screamed
and begged for mercy and—almost—surely
—crept through the still house doing mischief
while others slept.

The woman is inhuman! she thought with an
intensity that surprised her. But it was true,
there was something uncanny in her silence.
There she sat, ruffled and high-heeled as usual,
her sleek dark head poised, as though she were
at home on the chaise longue were she spent
so many idle hours.

Or perhaps they were not idle. Perhaps she
spent them weaving spells, Daphne thought. The

idea was so absorbing that she lost the thread of a story Mr. Whitney was telling, and could only nod when he waited for her answer. "I'm sorry. The scenery was distracting me!"

"Is this the first time you've been in the swamp country, Miss Summerfield? People are generally right interested in it, first time they see it."

She shivered. "It's—well, it's eerie."

The guest was enjoying the ride, at any rate. Although Isabel sat between them and took a lively part in the conversation, Daphne was only too conscious of his nearness and the glow in his eyes. She tried to hide her confusion by turning her attention to her pupil. "Where is your hat? You'll be sunburned."

"Oh, no, it's shady in the swamp."

They had ridden deeper and deeper into the wooded country, but it was not woodland such as she had known in Maine. The heat was damp and oppressive, the ground at once hummocky and swampy. Long streamers of gray moss hung from the branches of prehistoric-looking cypress and water oaks. Pale sunlight trickled through their matted boughs. At times the buggy wheels were almost hub-deep in water. Pools covered with greenish slime stood about.

Whitney laughed softly. "Don't you be one bit alarmed Miss Summerfield. We'll soon be at some kind of a landing and a pirogue will be waiting for us, I'll venture. These outings are quite safe and very pleasant, even if things do seem a little strange at first to a Yankee."

Charles said without turning around, "A pirogue and Miguel, as well as a boy to look after the horses until we return. This country only looks lonely, you know. There are farmers' and fishermen's shacks every here and there, but you'll never find them unless you know where they are."

"Miguel knows? A foreigner?"

"Miguel knows things that most people never learn."

Daphne couldn't help wondering what a pirogue was, but she felt that she had asked enough questions. She sat looking around her, not quite reassured. It was a strange country. Unfamiliar weeds and blossoms were matted together in a dense undergrowth. Bright trumpet-shaped flowers raised their heads above a tangle of verdure. Butterflies hovered over decaying stumps. She thought how it would be to get lost here, and shuddered.

Isabel asked, "What's the matter? Do you feel all right?"

"Of course."

"You'll love Hidden Island. When I grow up," Isabel said dreamily, "I'm going to build a shack on it and live there all the time, like the smugglers."

Charles said reasonably, "There haven't been any smugglers since the Lafitte Brothers worked out of New Orleans."

"Then maybe I'll be one, a lady smuggler. That would be more fun than keeping house, anyway."

The shadows grew deeper, the ground softer and spongier. It was a relief when they finally reached a wide stretch of water lying gray-green and oily looking between wooded banks. Miguel was there, his leathery face breaking into a smile of welcome as they came into sight. With him was a lanky boy of about fifteen, with ragged hair and a secretive face. "Cajun," Davis Whitney explained in a low voice.

"What is—"

"Supposed to be descended from the French settlers who were driven out of Canada, a long time ago. My history is a little vague, but it's true that they still speak a different kind of French from other people. You know, patois." He gave her a hand to dismount, and she stood looking around.

An odd boat was beached at the water's edge, with two pairs of wooden paddles in the bottom. Isabel followed her curious gaze. "Didn't you ever see a pirogue before?"

"We're going in *that*?"

"Of course. It's fun. The Cajuns say a pirogue can float on a heavy dew, and it's true; they go where even a canoe won't." Charles, having secured the horses, was handing baskets and bundles to Miguel. He added, "In the old days, pirogues were actually made of logs, hollowed out by burning and caulked to keep the water out. Some of them held ten or a dozen men, with supplies. Now they're made like other boats, but as you see, we've retained the original shape. It's the best craft for navigating these waters."

They were actually going somewhere in this insecure-looking craft. Davis Whitney stood protectively close, smiling. "You could paddle maybe a hundred, two hundred miles through the bayous, with a short portage now and then. There's a chain of them from here to the Gulf, I reckon. The trappers and fishermen know them like the palm of their own hands, but outsiders get lost mighty quickly. Many a good man has starved to death in these swamps, or been lost in the quicksands."

She could imagine them, long reaches of opaque water with unknown creatures hiding in their depths and swampy inlets reaching into the shoreline. Snakes and alligators, probably. As though her thoughts had materialized it, the largest turtle she had ever seen lifted its leathery neck and flat head from the water, looked around and lumbered up on land. She watched it disappear into the undergrowth.

The pirogue tipped frighteningly as Davis helped her in. Although he was a city man, he seemed quite at ease in this back country, seemed indeed to be enjoying himself. Charles and Miguel seated themselves at the bow and stern. The paddles dipped in rhythm. They were afloat. Pilar sat enthroned as if she were in her own drawing room. Daphne remembered that she had been a tomboy, paddling boats and climbing trees and fighting like a boy. Unlikely as it seemed, it at least explained the calm indifference with which she looked at the vague shores slipping past their craft.

Daphne looked across the murky water, hoping for a glimpse of dry land. The shoreline was uneven and dim in this strange half-light, with fingers of water reaching into the long grasses.

Long-legged birds stalked along the banks. Old gray trees stood up to their knobby knees in water. The bayou wound and twisted, with little mounds of island sticking up here and there. She tried to imagine two hundred miles of this, and knew that nothing would ever tempt her to set out on such a journey. Today's pleasure outing was taking all the courage of which she was capable.

She was glad when they reached the island, Charles' childhood playground. Davis helped her out of the boat. She lost her footing in the long damp grass and stood for a moment half falling, his firm grip on her arms keeping her upright. He was laughing good-naturedly, but she disengaged herself with all the dignity she could manage and held out her hands for one of the picnic baskets Miguel and Isabel were unloading. Safe on dry land, she started to giggle.

"Tell us the joke," Davis suggested.

"The Osbornes certainly choose some strange places for picnics. The last one was in the burying ground."

"We'll plan the next one at the back door," Charles promised her, "with Suzanne and the cookstove handy."

Davis filled her plate generously and sat down beside her on a fallen log, his own plate in one hand and a steaming mug on the ground within easy reach. It was the familiar strong black coffee. She shook her head when he offered her some. "There's a good red wine, too," he said, and leaned to reach the long-necked bottle.

Isabel said through a mouthful of ham, "After

lunch I'll show you where Papa and Tio Felipe used to have their tree house."

Pilar's face kindled into sudden animation. "And where we used to leave our magic letters, eh, Carlos? The ones written in invisible inks?"

Charles turned his head. "What?"

"You don't remember the summer when we wrote all those letters in invisible ink and left them in a cypress stump?"

He asked blankly, "Is it a joke? I never wrote you a letter in my life. You were my brother's girl from the time we were children."

For the second time in Daphne's presence, Pilar's voice rose loud and shrill. "Carlos, you are insane! Felipe and I fought like cats always, from the day my mother died and my father brought me home!" Her smooth face had turned a sick gray; her forehead creased with disbelief. "Sometimes I'm afraid of you." She turned to the others for support. "He has these attacks ever since he came back from Spain. He can't remember things; he says crazy things; he treats his wife as no sane man would think of doing! I think his head was hurt in that accident. I am afraid of him!"

In the silence that followed her outburst, Whitney put a protective arm around Daphne.

Charles said with an obvious effort, "Oh, those letters. We made the ink of lemon juice, didn't we?"

Pilar stared. Charles said airily, "You can't expect me to remember every detail of my childhood. Too much has happened since."

Pilar said in a venomous tone, "We were not

102

children. It was the summer before we married. But I have never meant much to you, especially since the world is full of other women—wishy-washy little things with blue eyes and doll faces. How stupid you are!"

Charles looked ill, but he kept his voice level. "Let's not have all this melodrama. Isabel, there's a pecan cake in the small basket. Do you think you can cut five slices without chopping off more than a finger or two?"

Isabel jumped up. Some of the tension evaporated. Miguel, sitting well away from the others but within easy reach of the hampers, took a bite from the drumstick he had been holding for at least ten minutes. Daphne moved out of the circle of Davis Whitney's arms, but the feeling of them stayed with her, warm and comforting.

Was Charles really out of his mind?

One slip meant nothing, of course. She had experienced the familiar annoyance of forgetting a friend's name, or mislaying some everyday object. But this was more serious. She knew from casual talk that Pilar and Philip Osborne had quarreled constantly as children and been at swords' points since reaching adult life. Philip had been opposed to his brother's early marriage, and she had never forgiven him. Then how could Charles say such a senseless thing?

This was not an absent-minded lapse. She feared it was an indication of something really wrong. Panicked, she looked at Charles. His strained face was more than she could bear. She turned her head, and met Davis Whitney's eyes.

It was evident that the little episode hadn't meant anything to him. He was thinking about her.

She knew that he saw her as small, helpless, appealing, a princess in a dark tower.

It would be easy to encourage him to come to her rescue. He was a good serious-minded man, for all his interest in dances and the theater. She felt quite sure that if she encouraged him a little, his dawning interest would develop into something deeper.

He could take her away from Fairlawn. Make her Mrs. Davis Whitney, with a home in New Orleans and a safe, comfortable life—indeed, a life more luxurious than she had ever dreamed of knowing. She would have a place in the society of America's most cosmopolitan and sophisticated city.

After all, what had she to look forward to? Granny was gone; the last tie with her own people broken. There was no place where she belonged. She could stay at Fairlawn until some mishap overtook her—she was sure, now, that something too dark for understanding was happening there. She recalled the opened window, the bitter tea, the shredded dress, and was afraid.

Or she could go back to Maine and become a spinster schoolmarm. Ahead of her stretched a long span of years with neither grief nor happiness to break their flat monotony.

Davis was a refuge. She liked him. Perhaps she could learn to love him. They would have children. His admiration for her was evident in every look he turned on her and every inflection of his voice when he spoke to her. All she had to do was fan the flame a little, and she could be Mrs. Davis Whitney.

I won't decide now, she thought. *It's too soon.*

Her eyes met Charles'. She felt strangely comforted by her decision. *I'll think about it all tonight,* she decided, *when I am alone. After all, marriage is not a matter to decide in haste.*

XIII

Dusk was settling over the countryside when they turned into the driveway between the great stone gateposts. Miguel, hunched over the reins, looked like a tired little gnome as he brought the horses to a stop. An air of weariness and relaxation pervaded the entire party.

Except for a few unpleasant moments, it had been an enjoyable day. Even Daphne was willing to forget her fears of the silent swamp and its hidden creatures; after all, she had yet to see an alligator. As for the quarrel at lunch, it had occurred to her that the Osbornes were perhaps used to these and did not mind them as much as other people might.

It was good to be at home again. She smiled, wryly, to realize that returning to Fairlawn was coming home even for her. She looked forward to being in her own room, where the mismatched bowl and pitcher offered refreshment and the plump bolster waited for her tired head. Left to herself, she would have escaped to quiet and privacy without more ado.

"I must admit I'll be sorry to leave tomorrow," Whitney said easily as they walked together toward the big house. "My stay has been right pleasant."

Charles said promptly, "Happy to have you here. Why don't you stay over a few days?"

"I'm sorry." The offer may have been intended only as a courtesy, but Davis' regret sounded real. "My mother is expecting me home on Sunday. We have guests arriving from France. Perhaps you'll let me come again." He looked questioningly at Daphne.

It was Pilar who answered, in all her dignity as hostess. "You are very welcome here, Mr. Whitney, any time that suits your convenience. If you can give us a few days' warning, we'll arrange to do some entertaining when you come again."

Daphne had never heard her speak so cordially to anyone. Nor had she suspected that the Osborne's relations with their neighbors were such as to make social functions possible. Pilar seemed to mean it, however. She added, "Suzanne will have a light supper ready for us in a few minutes. If you hope to take the morning train at Fairlawn Station, no doubt you will want to retire early."

She trailed her muslin ruffles across the dewy grass to the wide marble steps and vanished within the big front door, leaving the others in a small silent group.

Charles broke the silence. "Isabel, do you want to have a bite of supper with us, or shall Suzanne bring you some soup on a tray? You seem to be having a hard time keeping your eyes open. They have been closed most of the time since we started home."

"A tray, Papa. I want to go to bed and dream about Hidden Island."

Involuntarily, Daphne hoped that she would be spared the dream Isabel longed for. The island, or at least its approach, seemed more suitable material for a nightmare than for restful slumber.

The child stood on tiptoe and threw her arms around her father. "Oh, Papa, you're so nice. I love you much more now than when I was a little girl."

"Shows that you're getting smarter as you grow older," he assured her. "Now scat! Miguel tells me there are five new kittens in the stable. Tomorrow you may choose one to be your special pet."

"Can it sleep on my bed?"

"We'll see. Now, good night."

Miguel grasped the horses' bridles and turned them in the direction of the stables. He paused at Daphne's side. "Can you come to the stables, alone, *señorita*, while the others are waiting for dinner?"

She nodded. "I'll try."

It wasn't easy. Davis hovered close to her as they went indoors. She smiled sweetly at him. "Will you excuse me for a few minutes? I must say good night to Isabel, and I'd like to freshen up a bit."

"We'll be waiting for your return—and I must say you're pretty as a picture, just as you are."

Isabel was already in bed, her clothes a rumpled pile in the middle of the floor. She grinned cheerfully at Daphne, who decided not to mention her untidiness. After all, she was usually a responsible child. "Do you like my island, Miss Summerfield?"

"It's very interesting."

Isabel nodded, and buried her head in the pillow. Daphne waited a moment. She mumbled, "A gray kitten," and trailed off into silence. It was plain that Suzanne's tray wouldn't be needed. Daphne stooped to kiss her good night, half closed the door behind herself, and tiptoed down the back stairs.

The sound of voices drifted back from the drawing room, where the other members of the party were waiting for their supper. Daphne darted through the kitchen, where Suzanne with her usual unruffled air was quickly putting together a platter of cold meat and embellishing it with herbs. She nodded understandingly as the governess put a finger to her lips.

The outdoor air was cool. Daphne skimmed across the back yard, holding her skirt up to avoid the wet grass, and reached the stable. She reflected that she was not at all afraid to be outdoors alone at night. It was the sights and sounds in the big house that were alarming. But the dim light that shone out of the harness-room window was welcome. Breathing hard, she tapped on the door of the little room where Miguel slept and kept his few possessions.

The top half of the door swung open, and the old Spaniard looked out. Seeing her, he unlatched the lower panel and stood back to admit her to his private domain.

The five kittens he had mentioned were curled up in a box in the corner, their blind little faces turned toward the mother cat, who stood over them looking both anxious and proud. She watched Miguel with round yellow eyes as he stooped to pat her babies, but made no protest. Daphne asked him curiously, "How is it you get along so well with animals, Miguel? I don't mean only the farm animals. I've seen squirrels come up to you and talk, and they're afraid of most people."

The old man's seamed face was grave. "I have never harmed any living thing, *señorita*. The animals know their friends." He hesitated. "Only to save one I love would I do a violence."

She looked around the neat, primitive little room. Miguel cherished his privacy, she knew. She had not been here since her first visit with Isabel, the day after her arrival at Fairlawn. A lantern hanging on the wall shed a soft yellow light over the blanket-covered cot, the box of sleepy kittens and the clutter on the workbench. A bright glint caught her eyes. She walked over and picked up the shiny object. "Oh, it's your silver bullet! But you've smoothed and polished it, haven't you?"

"Yes. It is ready."

"Ready for what?"

"Who knows?" His face became a mask of caution. He took the bullet from her hand and placed it carefully in the drawer. "This young man from the city, he likes you. He is also of an age for courtship."

Daphne looked at the floor. "I scarcely know him."

"To fall in love takes no time. It is not a matter of the calendar, or even of the clock, but of the heart." Miguel chuckled. "If you married him, he could take you far from this place."

This was so close to her own thoughts of the afternoon that she could only stare at him, the color rising in her cheeks. Making an effort to regain her composure, she said coldly, "I don't think that concerns you. Anyway, he hasn't spoken of marriage. I have no reason to believe that he's thinking of any such thing."

"Ah, the lady decides these things. She holds him off or beckons him to come closer, even when there is a duenna as in my country," Miguel said wisely. "He will speak if you want him to, and if you do not want it, then he will go away without speaking."

Daphne said with all the dignity she could manage, "I must go to the house now. Suzanne is preparing supper."

He put a hand on her arm. The gesture was so fatherly that she could not resent it. "I am sorry if you are angry, Doña Daphne. I must tell you one thing, even if it makes you more angry. Do not be afraid of my master. He is not mad. If all the world were as sane as he, it would be well. He will do no harm to you or anyone else."

He added smiling, "The squirrels and birds talk with him, too."

She said untruthfully, "I'm not afraid of anyone. Or anything."

"I saw fear in your eyes today," Miguel said simply. "I have seen it there before. There is much to fear in this world, but not from a good man." He hesitated. "My master cannot tell all, because it would do harm to others, but you must believe that he is in his right mind, and do not be afraid."

He was so intense that she had to forgive him. Whatever lay behind his outburst, it was meant to reassure her. And she did feel less apprehensive, foolish as that might be. Whatever Charles' secret might be, Miguel knew him better than she did, and she had already learned that the old groom was a shrewd judge of character.

She smiled at him. "Thank you Miguel. And now I must go back, before they miss me."

She slipped quietly into the house and tiptoed to the dining room, where the sound of dishes and voices indicated that the informal meal was already under way. Too late, she realized that her low shoes and the edge of her skirt were wet from the grass, and her hair still untidy. No help for it—Davis Whitney had already caught sight of her in the doorway. He jumped up to welcome her. She took her place quickly, hoping that none of the others had noticed her disarray."

Charles said, "I gather that Isabel is asleep?"

"Dreaming about her island and her plans to be a smuggler, I think."

Davis said warmly, "She is a delightful little girl; she reminds me of my youngest sister. You must be sure to bring her if you come to New Orleans this autumn." He spoke directly to Daphne, although he had already made it plain that the invitation included all of them. "My father and mother will be happy to be your hosts when the rice is harvested—of course it will be impossible to get Charles away before then! And I hope to see you long before that, if I haven't worn out my welcome."

Pilar said, "You will find a welcome here at any time, Mr. Whitney. Do you not agree, Miss Summerfield?"

"Of course," Daphne stammered, "but after all, it's not my house."

"But you are the attraction," Pilar said sweetly.

"Will you have a little sherry before your dinner, Miss Summerfield?" Charles' tone was that of a good host. Daphne shook her head. "No, thank you. I see that the rest of you have begun your dinner—and I'm too drowsy to be hungry, anyway."

"Then we'll all retire early," Davis said pleasantly. His eyes told her that she was indeed, as Pilar said, the attraction, but that it was necessary to include these other people in the conversation. Simply a matter of courtesy. If he came back to Fairlawn, it would be her presence that drew him there.

She had spoken truthfully when she said that she was tired. But when the little party separated and she found herself alone in her room, she was unable to sleep.

She blew out the single candle by whose flickering light she had undressed, and opened the curtain that covered the window. The moon had risen, and its clear white light flooded the lawn and sparkled on the long drive. Remembering that she was in her short-sleeved night-dress, with her hair loose on her shoulders, she placed a small chair well back from the window and sat where no lurking observer could see her. Not that there was any sign of life anywhere in that grassy expanse, but still—

She felt deeply troubled, and at the same time oddly happy. Perhaps, she thought, she had been working too hard. A day in the open air had driven away some of the nervous fancies that troubled her, and restored her usual good spirits.

She had still to deal with the question of Davis Whitney. Was his admiration a problem or a solution? Even within the limits of a small New England village, she had observed enough of love and courtship to know that his feeling for her, still in its beginning stages, was sincere. He was not the man to trifle with an innocent girl under the roof and protection of a man he respected, or seduce an orphan in straitened circumstances. She was sure that his intentions, when he became aware of them, would be honorable.

The question was not whether he would propose, given a chance, but whether she wanted him to. Miguel had been right when he declared that the course of a courtship was in the hands of the woman. But why had he followed it with a defense of Charles?

She felt confused and a little frightened.

The hands of her bedside clock stood at half-past eleven when she finally drew the heavy curtain, first making sure that the window was open only its usual cautious two inches. After all the day's excitement, it would hardly be surprising if she walked in her sleep.

Stretching out in her wide bed, she hoped with all her heart that no one else would be walking tonight. Neither Pilar in her elaborately furnished room at the far end of the hall, nor Charles from the smaller chamber that he and his brother had shared as boys, nor any supernatural being bent on evil. *If there are ghosts,* she thought with a giggle, *I'm too sleepy tonight to pay any attention to them.*

She had still not come to any decision about Davis Whitney. *After all,* she thought as a pleasant drowsiness crept over her, *he can scarcely propose at the breakfast table, and by the time he pays his next visit to Fairlawn, I'll have come to some conclusion.* She wondered whether the Osbornes would really pay a visit to New Orleans if the rice crop brought a large enough sum.

The house was quiet, except for the little creakings and sighings that old houses make as they settle, and the tiny squeaking of a mouse in the wall in a tree outside her window, a small bird chirped sleepily.

She turned over and fell deeply and dreamlessly asleep, more at peace than she had been since she left the shelter of her grandmother's house.

XIV

For the first time since her arrival at Fairlawn, Daphne found herself looking forward to Charles' weekly trips to the nearest town. She did not have the courage to suggest that she would like to accompany him, although on her visit to Dr. Perron she had been interested in the sleepy little village just because it was so unlike the places she had known. The thought of Pilar's cool surprised stare kept her from asking, as well as the reminder of her conscience that she was there as Isabel's teacher and companion and was not free to go riding around the countryside for her own pleasure.

Davis Whitney's first letters arrived five days after his departure from the plantation. Charles, coming into the drawing room rather paler and more silent than usual, handed one envelope to Pilar and the other to Daphne. "The young man seems to be quite a letter writer," he said with an attempt to smile.

Daphne took hers curiously. The envelope was square, so stiff and heavy that it crackled in her hand, and the address was written in heavy black script. She turned it over. It was sealed with a wafer of dark-red wax into which an intricate design had been pressed. "Seal ring," Charles said, catching her inquiring look. "Family crest, most likely."

Pilar was reading quickly through her missive. Her slightly slanted eyes came to rest on the governess. "Another bread and butter letter for you?" she asked, too gently. "But you were not his hostess."

Daphne made no move to open her envelope. She half feared and half hoped that it was, indeed, only a polite note with no personal implications. *But it's mine,* she reminded herself. *I have a right to read it when I like.*

She turned the letter over. The seal made Davis seem more like a stranger. She had never known anyone who had a family crest, or wrote on such heavy expensive-looking paper.

Charles said in the firm way he could assume on occasion, "You will read your mail in the privacy of your own chamber, of course. We will see you at lunch."

She flashed him a grateful smile, but the letter seemed to burn into her palm as she carried it upstairs. Not until she reached the top did she realize that Pilar's expression had been pleased, if cool. The older woman was glad that she had heard from Whitney. But why?

She closed the door of her bedroom behind her and slit the envelope. A single sheet of heavy paper fell out, covered in the same firm writing.

"*My dear Miss Summerfield,*
"*I have just written to thank the Osbornes for the welcome which they so kindly ten-*

116

dered to me last week. It was indeed a pleasure to partake of their hospitality. May I say, without offensive familiarity, that not the least of my enjoyment was the opportunity of becoming acquainted with you, and of undertaking a friendship which I venture to hope will be of lengthy duration and increasing happiness to both parties concerned.

"Please bear in mind that my parents hope, as I do, for the pleasure of a visit from you in late October or November, when Mr. Osborne is able to absent himself from the responsibilities of the plantation for a few days. Until that time I shall continue writing to you, with your kind permission, unless I hear from your own hand that such a hope meets with your displeasure. I shall hope for a few lines from you whenever you have the leisure to take your pen in hand.

Respectfully yours,
Davis Beaumarchais Whitney"

She sat for a while with the paper in her hand, her mind in a turmoil.

The letter confirmed what she had already suspected, that Davis was seriously attracted to her. Through the formal lines shone the eagerness of a young man intent upon wooing a girl. Each phrase had been carefully chosen to further his suit. She had found the right word—it was indeed the letter of a suitor.

She asked herself whether she wanted a suitor, and found no answer.

She knew that the situation was unusual. A penniless governess with no family and no prospects, no refuge even if illness or destitution overtook her, she was being gently but firmly urged toward the sort of marriage that she and her girlhood friends had dreamed of in their most romantic moments. If she said "yes" to the proposal that would surely be forthcoming in the autumn, her life would take on the soft rosy glow of those novels that Granny publicly disapproved of and secretly enjoyed reading.

The big house at Fairlawn had taken her breath away the first time she saw it, even though its splendor was marred by decay and neglect. She knew that the Whitney House on Prytania Street in New Orleans would be, if not as large, elegantly and lavishly furnished and maintained in a state of near perfection. The life that went on in those spacious rooms would not be hindered by financial worries and the vagaries of an eccentric mistress, like life at Fairlawn, but always easy and enjoyable. Davis Whitney's wife would have invitations to balls and dances, concerts and plays. She would command a retinue of servants, a carriage and horses, and in her armoire would hang the finest silks and laces from the great Paris designers. All these things would be hers through the devoted love of a fine man and the security of a closely-knit family circle.

Davis had described the gown his mother had worn to a Mardi Gras ball, the year before.

Ashes-of-roses satin from Worth, packed so carefully in Paris that when the maid shook it out after the long ocean voyage there was not a single wrinkle in the heavy material. "With it she wore the string of pearls which every Beaumarchais bride receives from her betrothed on the wedding night, the clasp of sapphires and diamonds to match the sapphire and diamond ring with which my father sealed their troth." He added proudly, "She is still a very beautiful woman. My father plans to have her portrait painted by Sargent next year, to hang in the salon."

Brought up in the New England tradition of industry and thrift, she knew that a lifetime of unremitting toil would not bring her even one of the luxuries that would belong to young Mrs. Davis Whitney without any effort on her part.

She liked him, would have liked him even without all these mundane considerations. She told herself, miserably truthful, that she would have liked him as a brother. As do most only children, she had always dreamed of having a brother. But when she thought of a man's embrace, it was another face that rose in her mind—a face too old for its years, lined with worry and fatigue.

She pushed the vision away, and with it the memory of a pair of sheltering arms lifting her to the carriage seat. She had no right to feel this way about a man who was irrevocably married to another woman.

As on several other occasions since the handsome young Orleanian had come into her life, she reminded herself that it was too soon to make a decision. She would wait and see what the future brought.

Still, as the hot days of late summer passed she found herself looking forward to Friday's mail. There was sure to be one of the heavy square envelopes among the stack of magazines and papers that Charles insisted on subscribing to, even though Pilar objected that he couldn't afford them. Usually it was the only letter, unless someone wrote to him on plantation business. She gathered that the death of the Spanish uncle had put a stop to all communication with Don Jaime's family. Perhaps they felt, understandably enough, that his American stepsons were of no interest to his relatives. Pilar had no family unless you counted the bands of swarthy gypsies roaming over Spain and Portugal, singing, dancing, telling fortunes, stealing. Brought to Don Jaime upon her mother's death and by man to the New World, she had no connections with anyone.

"My mother's kinfolks write once a year, at Christmas," Charles said, seeming to read Daphne's thoughts as he so often did. He found her letter between the *Times-Democrat* and *Harper's Magazine,* and handed it to her. "Most southern families have hundreds of kissin' cousins, and it's a rare Virginian who has no one at all."

"Papa, you have me!" Isabel, waiting for the small surprise her father usually brought back from Saint Laurent in an inside pocket, jumped up and flung her arms around him. He looked at Daphne over the top of her bright head. "I hope so, kitten."

"Can I ride to town with you the next time you go?"

"If Miss Summerfield will excuse you from your lessons."

"Oh, that's nothing. I learn quick-quick."

Daphne said, "It's true; she has been working very hard."

"Then you may come with me next week, if Miss Summerfield says so. What's the attraction in Saint Laurent?"

"Oh, Papa, Mr. Jackson's store! There is some of everything in the world there, and the Jackson children know all the games there are. There's no one here to play with—except Miss Summerfield," she added politely, "and she's too old."

A smile lit Charles' face. "Yes, I can see that Miss Summerfield is a tottering old lady. Perhaps she—"

He broke off, his smile vanishing. Daphne finished the sentence in her own mind, "—*would like to go along.*"

"—will be glad to do without you for a few hours."

She was disappointed, but she managed not to show it. There would still be the weekly letter to look forward to, as well as the periodicals, which Charles had placed at her disposal. Pilar never opened a paper, nor for that matter any of the dignified leather-bound volumes that filled the library shelves. They had become her favorite means of passing the long sultry afternoons when even Isabel consented to rest and Pilar disappeared until dinner time.

Late in September, when the rice was heading out and the summer heat began to seem endless, Davis wrote the Osbornes to say that he would be in their part of the state the following week and would like, if they found it convenient, to pay them a short visit. He would arrive on Wednesday and take his leave on Friday. "Since I have been offered the use of a carriage and team by my mother's second cousin, Alcide Beaumarchais of Saint Jean Baptiste Parish, I need not ask Charles to interrupt his work in the fields." The letter ended on a practical note. "I may say that if the weather holds, conditions look most favorable for the growers. The crop is good, but not so large as to bring prices down, and your rice, *mon cher* Charles, compares favorably with the best I have seen this season. I give the credit to your constant supervision, which has kept your field hands industrious and alert."

There was nothing in all this business talk to make Daphne's heart flutter, but she was a little breathless all the same as she opened her own missive. It was shorter than usual. "As Mr. and Mrs. Osborne no doubt have told you, I hope to be at Fairlawn next week. I have an important question which I shall ask you at that time, with your permission."

There was no doubt in her mind as to what the important question would concern. She replaced the letter in its envelope and put it between the pages of Granny's well-worn Bible, on the bedside table.

All through lunch, which was more hurried than usual, she was torn between conflicting feelings of anticipation and dread. What would she say to him? She had not expected to have to make a decision so soon, and now the time she had both waited for and dreaded was at hand.

I wish I had something new to wear, she thought as she climbed the stairs to her own room after the meal. *Something of my own, not borrowed finery.* Shivering she remembered in vivid detail the dinner at which she had worn the blue silk dress, and her horrifying discovery of its shredded remnants the next morning.

Reminded of the ruined gown, she decided that she would dispose of it that very afternoon. Isabel, pleading that it was too cool for a siesta, was off for a canter with Miguel. In the old neglected orchard behind the house she had noticed a huge hollow stump half filled with decaying leaves. It would be easy to push a bundle of ruined silk into the cavity and cover it over.

She tiptoed past the closed door behind which Pilar was presumably taking a siesta, and shut herself into her own room. Flinging open the carved doors of the wardrobe, she reached behind the modest row of dresses for the roll of blue silk.

It was gone.

Sure that she had forgotten exactly where she put it, she drew the window curtains wide open.

Strong afternoon sunshine poured in, revealing every detail of the room and its furnishings in sharp relief.

She pushed her dresses aside and looked again. The remains of the blue silk evening gown had vanished as completely as though they had never existed.

Bewildered, she pushed her hair back from a forehead suddenly damp with nervous perspiration. *Maybe I dreamed the whole thing,* she thought. *Maybe I'm out of my mind.*

For a moment she was willing to believe that the whole thing had been a nightmare, that she had actually hung the dress back on Doña Camilla's wardrobe. But were dreams and reality ever so inseparable, once one was awake?

Resisting an impulse to invade the closed and shuttered corner room and see if the dress were indeed hanging there among the others, she sat down on the edge of the bed.

At least, she thought, *I didn't imagine Davis. He was really here, and he has written to me every week. He will be here, at Fairlawn, next Wednesday. I must decide how warm a welcome I want to give him, and what my answer to his "important question" will be.*

She reached for the little leather-bound Bible, to reassure herself by rereading his letter that he actually existed and would soon be with her.

The letter, too, was gone.

XV

Heavy-eyed after a night of broken sleep, she descended the wide stairs the next morning. She had lain awake for a long time, going over and over all the strange happenings of her stay at Fairlawn. The fears of her first weeks, which had receded from her mind since meeting Davis, came to life again and seemed to crowd around her bed, taunting her. When she dozed at last, it was to dream of weird creatures with fangs and burning eyes howling outside her window, and silent phantoms gliding through the corridors of the old house.

Waked at last by her own terror, she lay wide-eyed in the early morning light, trying to piece together the events that had brought her to this sleepless state.

She was not encouraged to discover that the air was heavy and the sky overcast, when at last she got out of bed and prepared to meet the day. Without sunshine, the countryside looked alien and threatening. She went downstairs slowly, reluctant to spend the day indoors and knowing that Isabel, too, would be unruly because her daily ride must be postponed. She opened the door of the little morning room where she and her pupil were in the habit of taking their breakfast.

This morning the round table was set for three. Isabel, her hair still tangled from the night's sleep, was eating hot biscuits and black-berry jam with her usual healthy appetite. Across the table, her father sipped black coffee and listened to her chatter about the horse she was riding later in the day. He looked up with a slight frown as Daphne opened the door. Isabel broke off in mid-sentence. "Oh, Miss Summerfield, I've been waiting for you! Papa has to go to Saint Laurent this morning. May I go along?"

Her plan for a new dress revived. "I don't see why not. As a matter of fact, I have some shopping to do, too. If there's room for two passengers—"

"I was planning to take the light buggy. Have to get a part for the reaper; those boys always break things at the most inconvenient time. But come along, if you think you can find anything you want in Saint Laurent. Isabel can ride along some other time."

"Oh, Papa, there's room for three in the light buggy."

"If you don't mind elbows in your ribs."

Isabel scowled. Then her face cleared. "All right. Miguel promised to take me out if it doesn't rain. He's teaching me to ride sidesaddle like a lady."

Did she imagine it, or did he look relieved? "You stay close to Miguel and do whatever he tells you, and you'll be all right. I think the rain will pass over."

Concerned with the sky and her last-minute shopping list, it was not until she found herself perched on the high buggy seat, close enough to be aware of his breathing, that Daphne was assailed by any qualms about the propriety of setting out on a trip alone with another woman's husband. She folded her hands primly in her lap and looked away from him, afraid that he would be able to read her thoughts if she met his eyes.

"What's the matter?"

"I was just wondering—I mean, I don't know the customs here—I mean—"

Charles chuckled. "Are you afraid of me or of the neighbors?"

"Neither." The answer came promptly. Whatever doubts she may have felt in his absence, it was impossible to distrust him now.

He said slowly, "I don't want to offend any maidenly modesty you may have, but could I remind you that we drove to Saint Laurent alone the day you sprained your ankle?" His eyes twinkled. "In fact, if I remember rightly, I carried you to the buggy and propped you up in the seat."

Her blush deepened. "That was an emergency."

"So is this. If I don't get hold of the right size bolt, the early rice is going to pass its prime before we get it husked and under cover. And judging from the shadows under your eyes, I'd say that you are having problems of your own. Anything really wrong?"

"No. Oh, I don't know!" Suddenly the entire fantastic chain of events seemed more than she could endure alone. She had to tell someone of her fears. *Maybe there's a reasonable explanation for everything,* she thought hopefully. *May-*

be he can make it all clear to me. She began timidly, "Do you remember the blue silk dress I wore to dinner one evening?"

She was prepared for laughter, or even anger, but not for the wary look that came over his face. She wished that she had never brought the matter up. Now there didn't seem to be any way of stopping. She blundered on, telling him about the discovery of the mutilated remnants the next morning and hiding them in her wardrobe. "And yesterday, when I remembered it and went to take it away, there was nothing there."

Of course, she thought as her voice died away, *he won't believe a word of it. He'll think I'm out of my mind. And perhaps I am.*

He asked dully, "Have there been other things? Things that frightened you?"

Slowly, she told him about the opened window. "And that's how I sprained my ankle. Of course, Suzanne may have opened it to air the room, and forgotten to close it again."

"It must have been frightening to wake and find yourself hanging over twenty feet of nothingness."

For a split second, she felt again the vertigo that engulfed her when she realized that she was teetering over an abyss. "The veranda is directly below my window, you know." She added hastily, "I check it every night now. It's all right."

There was a silence. She looked away from him, across the flat fields, torn between her desire to tell him the rest—the tea episode, and Miguel's warnings concerning witches and the evil eye—and her realization that she could hardly do so without seeming to accuse Pilar. Worse, she would have to admit that for a short time she had even doubted him. It was an impossible confession. She pressed her lips together and looked away from him.

"There's more." It was a statement rather than a question.

"Nothing important."

He said carefully, abandoning the formality that had marked their talk until now, "Daphne, listen to me. I don't know everything that is happening at Fairlawn—there are things I don't understand. But I can promise you one thing. No harm will come to you if I can prevent it. You have my word for that."

His tone was graver than the words could account for. Tears came to her eyes. She blinked to hold them back, but two crystal globes spilled over and rolled down the bosom of her blouse. Without another word, he pulled a rumpled handkerchief out of his pocket and handed it to her.

They were silent the rest of the way. She was glad when they left the open fields behind and drove between a double row of tumbledown shacks in whose yards ragged children, black and white, were quarreling and playing. These soon gave way to respectable houses with tree-shaded yards, and then to the main street she recalled from her earlier visit. The bony old men sitting and whittling outside the store could have been the same ones, undisturbed since her first glimpse of them.

Charles pulled the horse to a stop at the iron

hitching post and helped her down. Now that she was here, she felt conspicuous and shy. Two large women in slatted sunbonnets passed, then turned back to look at her. *It's only because I am a stranger*, she told herself. *Small-town people are always curious.*

The shadowy interior of the store was cool and quiet, redolent of freshly roasted coffee and coal oil and pickles and half a dozen other things, rather pleasantly blended. As the counters and barrels emerged from the general gloom she looked around, fascinated. One side of the room was given to groceries, the other dry goods and miscellaneous merchandise, but they had overflowed and become mixed. A pile of rubber boots lay on a counter next to several boxes of salted fish, and the shelves held bottles of Peruna and Father John's Medicine as well as bolts of cloth and sewing supplies. She hesitated, wondering how she would ever find anything in such a jumble.

Her anxiety was groundless. Stout Mrs. Jackson came out of the back room, fluttering, ignoring a sunbonneted mother with two barefoot little girls who was comparing the merits of blue-checked gingham with gray-sprigged calico. Evidently the quality received prior attention here, and the Fairlawn governess was quality by association, at least. A little embarrassed, Daphne answered as many of Mrs. Jackson's questions as she could and then selected a length of lawn with tiny pink and blue flowers on a white ground, narrow lace for the neck and sleeves, and sewing essentials. Remembering Isabel's disappointment, she also bought a sack of chocolate creams —not a wise choice, as she realized when they began to melt under the hot sun, on the way home.

"Won't you have a small black with us? Mr. Jackson's always glad to drop his work and talk to Mr. Osborne."

"Not today, I'm afraid. The hands are waiting for a machine part. May I come and see you some other time?"

"Of course, my dear. I reckon it's lonely way out there in the country, away from everything." She looked shrewdly at Daphne. Uncertain whether or not she meant more than appeared on the surface, the girl managed to answer cheerfully, "Oh, no, I like the country."

"Have you found everything you need?" Charles came up behind her and took her parcels. She had not heard him enter the store. "Please give my greetings to Mr. Jackson, Mrs. Jackson. It's surely a pleasure to see you again."

He had her outside almost before she could make her farewells. "A great gossip, but she has a heart as big as a washtub," he said good-naturedly, glancing back at the little store with its wide sagging veranda. Not for the first time, she realized that she was being managed and not minding it. When occasion required, this quiet man could put himself in charge of a situation quickly and surely.

Except, she thought suddenly, where his own wife was concerned. In her presence he was courteous but guarded, moving quietly and saying little. It seemed a strange way for a husband of eleven years' standing to behave, but then, Pilar was hardly an ordinary wife.

Thinking of Pilar, she felt apprehensive again. What if she were angry, or coldly scornful as she so often seemed to be, because Daphne had ridden along to Saint Laurent? *I should have asked her*, she thought. And then, angrily independent, *Oh, nonsense. I've been on call day and night for three months. Even a housemaid is entitled to her day off.*

But a housemaid didn't spend her day off riding around the country with her employer, confiding silly fears and misgivings that she might better keep to herself.

It was the voice of conscience, and she had no answer. She sat silent the rest of the way home, clutching the crochet purse that still held most of her earnings. At least there was no temptation to be extravagant in Saint Laurent!

Lunch was waiting when they reached Fairlawn. Isabel came bouncing in, rumpled and happy from her morning on horseback, and the three of them went into the dining room where Pilar was already seated at the long table, waiting for them.

She was smiling. Daphne, startled, realized that she had never seen her employer's wife smile before, except as a social gesture. She asked pleasantly, "Did you find anything worth buying?"

Daphne collected her scattered thoughts. "Yes, thank you. I bought some flowered lawn to make a dress."

"I have been thinking," Pilar said brightly, "it's a long time since we have done any entertaining. Why not have a few of the neighbors in to meet Mr. Whitney? And Miss Summerfield, too," she added as though she had just thought of it. "It has been very dull for her here. We could get some of the local people in to help Suzanne, and perhaps have a little music after dinner."

Charles seated Daphne at the table before he answered. She had the feeling that he was trying to gain time. "I think it's an excellent idea," he said cheerfully, shaking out his napkin. "As you say, it has been a long time. We haven't given a party since, let me see—"

"Not since you came back from Spain."

"Has it really been that long? We could invite the Langleys, the Butlers, the Boulangers, Amédée Raquin and his mother—well, you make a list, and Miguel can deliver the invitations." He helped himself from the platter that Suzanne was holding at his elbow, ignoring her look of wide-eyed surprise.

"One thing more," Pilar said in the same pleasant tone, turning to Daphne. "I don't believe that you have a suitable gown for a formal dinner. If you are not too proud to wear someone else's clothes"—her lips twitched, and Daphne was reminded painfully of the only time she had ever decked herself out in borrowed finery—"I'll be glad to give you a dress that you can make over. You are clever with a needle, I know."

Daphne looked at Charles. There was no help for her there; he was intent upon his plate. She looked full at Pilar. The older woman's eyes were narrowed; her lips had a twist of ironic amusement. She reminded Daphne of a watchful cat, waiting for the mouse to venture out of its hiding place.

Daphne lifted her chin proudly. She was trembling, but her voice was steady. "Thank you, but I prefer not to borrow anything. I'll have my lawn dress finished in time for the party."

"A flowered lawn from Saint Laurent?"

"I can think of nothing more suitable for a young girl in modest circumstances," Daphne answered coolly. "If it is not good enough, I can stay in my room while you are entertaining your guests."

Pilar's eyes dropped. She turned away and began to eat her lunch.

Daphne, too, turned her attention to her plate of chicken and rice. Without knowing exactly what the issue was or why it had arisen, she was aware that for the first time, she had met Pilar in open combat and come off victorious.

XVI

Plans and preparations for the party filled most of Daphne's waking hours for the next few days. Since Suzanne was unable to give directions to the two local women who came to clean and refurbish the house, she assumed the duties of a housekeeper in addition to her daily supervision of Isabel's studies. It was a difficult task, because the thick dialect they spoke was almost as hard to understand as a foreign language of which she could pick out only a word here and there. But they were cheerful and willing, and under her direction they brought the old house to a state of shining beauty such as she had never dreamed it could assume. The cleaning that she and Suzanne had done before was only a preparation.

Fine old lace curtains were taken down and carefully laundered; antique rugs were sponged with ammonia solution to freshen their dimmed colors, the furniture was rubbed to a dark luster with homemade polish. Cakes were baked and iced, and Suzanne brought out from some hiding place a yellowed notebook with recipes for trifle and syllabub in "Miss Camilla's" Spencerian hand. Charles rode into Saint Laurent and brought back a new-fangled ice cream freezer which Suzanne quickly learned to operate.

Miguel put on his seldom-worn bottle green livery and rode off to deliver Charles' hand-written invitations to such of the gentry as lived within a radius of twenty miles or so. "Neighbors" in this thinly settled country seemed to include every of acceptable social rank within a day's ride. It was a new idea for a girl from a land of small rocky farms and snug villages, but she could understand why people went far afield to maintain their social contacts.

For the first time since her arrival at Fairlawn, she began to understand what life on a plantation must have been in the opulent days of the South. The entire atmosphere of the place changed as footsteps and cheerful Negro voices rang through its halls, where a mysterious silence had prevailed for so long. She had not realized how still the house was, or how gloomy were the dignified old rooms into which the sunshine was now streaming.

With so much to do, it was difficult to find any time for her own concerns. Falling into bed tired, after a day of not only supervising but participating in the preparations, she reminded herself that it was Pilar who ought to be doing all this; it was Pilar who was the mistress of this big old house, even though she ignored her duties as a chatelaine when there was no guest. But then she was thankful for a respite from her anxieties, as well as from the mysterious danger which had hung over her in the first weeks of her stay. Weariness was better than fear.

With Isabel's delighted help, she got the flowered lawn cut out, fitted and stitched. She was sure that Pilar would greet her guests in an elaborate gown of heavy silk, cut to flatter her bosom and round arms, and that her cotton frock would look dowdy by comparison. However, the girlish simplicity of the material, as well as her natural modesty, dictated a less revealing pattern for herself. She decided on a round neckline and short puffed sleeves that would have been suitable for Isabel, edged with frills of narrow lace. The skirt was full, and the pink taffeta sash from her Sunday dress, washed and ironed by Suzanne's skilled hands, would set off a pliant waist. Worn with her low-heeled white slippers and the gold locket which was her only ornament, it would be a becoming costume, if not an impressive one.

She hung the flowered dress carefully in her wardrobe, remembering the fate of the blue silk as she did so. But for the time being the curse that hung over Fairlawn, whatever it was, seemed to have been suspended.

The only mishaps were a loss of a sterling silver fork with the Ramirez crest, and the upsetting of a kettle of scalding water over the feet of one of the temporary helpers. Suzanne's tealeaf poultice soon eased the agony of the blistered flesh, and the woman was back at the kitchen table, blanching almonds and pleased to be the center of so much attention.

Daphne decided that the social isolation of the Osbornes, which had raised so many questions in her mind, was after all not due to any unfriendly spirit on the part of their neighbors. Acceptances in copperplate script followed Miguel's delivery of the invitations. Perhaps, after all, it was only Charles' dawn-to-dark activity on the plantation and Pilar's indolence and lack of interest in other people that had kept their friends away. In addition to Davis Whitney and the family, there would be twelve dinner guests. Seventeen in all, since Isabel was to stay up and dine with them.

"Teach her some manners," Charles said cheerfully. Daphne, with her heart pounding, wished that she were as confident of her own table etiquette as of Isabel's. Granny had taught her to behave like a lady under all circumstances, but so many of the heavy forks and spoons she helped Suzanne polish were unfamiliar to her. What did you eat with a tiny two-pronged fork, or cut with a saw-edged knife too small to separate a piece of meat?

She remembered that the hostess would be served first, and then the lady at Charles' right. By watching them, she hoped that she might get through the evening without disgracing herself.

With so many other things to think about, it was easy to put off all consideration of Davis Whitney. Even though all this activity was for his benefit, it was hard to remember what he looked like, or the sound of his voice. She wondered at her own indifference. Here was a man not only handsome and wealthy but of the highest character, with serious intentions concerning herself, and she could not even decide what answer she could give to his "important question."

It was all she could do, these evenings, to keep her eyes open through the long formally served dinners which were the only concessions the Osbornes made to a way of life that had been customary with their parents. She learned to choke down the "small black" that finished the meal, hoping that its stimulating effects would keep her awake until she could get to her own room.

She was startled out of her unthinking activity on Wednesday afternoon, when a smart rig and two sleek bays turned in at the lone lane. Miguel hobbled out to hold the horses and greet the traveler. A well-dressed young man with smooth dark hair alighted and stood in the sunshine, smiling as he answered the old servant's greeting. Daphne, standing in the doorway, thought with a shock of happy recognition, "Why, it's Davis!" As though she had known him for a long time, as though he were an old friend arrived unexpectedly.

She smoothed her hair, glad that she had put on a fresh blouse and white wash skirt, seeing herself through his frankly admiring eyes as he mounted the wide marble steps. She knew that even in this simple garb he found her beautiful and desirable. She reminded herself sternly that nothing was settled between them as yet, and that she was not sure what decision she would make in regard to him. Smiling, she allowed him to take her hand.

She was grateful for the presence of Isabel, who forgot all her adult mannerisms in the excitement of the meeting and welcomed him with the frank pleasure of a happy puppy. She liked the way he spoke to Isabel, giving her all his attention while he shook hands with her. He would be a good father. Not for the first time, she sighed over her own foolish indecision. Here was a man who combined the dash and glamour of a fairy-tale prince with those solid virtues she had been brought up to seek in a husband, and she could not make up her mind to accept him. *I'm behaving very stupidly*, she thought.

She came out of her reverie to realize that Isabel had led them to the cool drawing room and that one of the temporary maids was offering her a glass from a well-polished silver tray. She took one of the tall frosty drinks and buried her nose in the bush of mint that topped it, refusing to look at Davis until she could regain her composure.

The first sip of the amber liquid was like fire.

She suppressed a cough, and for the first time looked at Davis. He said pleasantly, "Charles writes that we are to have a gala evening. I hope that Miss Isabel will be allowed to stay up for the festivities."

"We're going to have dancing after dinner," Isabel told him joyously. "They moved the little piano into the drawing room, and old Uncle Berl from Maison Blanc is coming over with his fiddle. He has two friends who play the banjo and guitar, too. Will you dance with me, Mr. Whitney?"

The young man's voice was cordial, but his gaze was fixed on Daphne as he replied, "Of course. I look forward to it with the greatest pleasure. I'm positive that all of your friends are delightful people, but you and Miss Summerfield will surely be the belles of the ball."

Daphne was not sure whether it was his flattery or her second sip of bourbon that made her feel suddenly light and free. She said confidently, "Thank you, sir. Will you dance with me as well?"

His look was all the answer she needed.

XVII

Why hasn't anyone ever told me what a help wine is? Daphne wondered. She set down her glass, turned her head carefully (everything seemed to be floating in a soft haze) and looked around the great oaken table.

Tonight, for the first time in her weeks at Fair-lawn, it glittered with polished silver and rows of crystal glasses, fine porcelain and heavy damask overlaid with lace. Around its circumference the guests were dividing their attention between a plethora of elaborate desserts, the fine French champagne that Charles had brought up in cob-webbed bottles from his stepfather's wine cellar, and several conversations that seemed to begin and end lightly, like snatches of music hummed at random. Indeed, the easy drawl of the guests, set off by a crisp comment from Charles now and then, gave the scattered talk a melodious effect.

Something odd but rather pleasant had happened to her vision. Soft-colored blurs alternated with black and white ones around the table: the evening clothes of the ladies and those of the men. She managed to focus on Davis, at whose right hand Pilar had unexpectedly placed her. At this close range she could make out his features well enough. He was listening with courteous interest to old Mrs. Boulanger seated across the table. Daphne had no idea what they were talking about, for in her pleasure at finding someone who spoke fluent French the dignified old lady had lapsed into her accustomed tongue. In the flickering light from the half-burned candles Davis was more handsome than ever. His face was a little flushed with food and drink, but he seemed to be in command of the situation and enjoying himself thoroughly.

The manservant who had appeared in the dining room at the beginning of the meal was at her elbow, napkin-swathed bottle tipped invitingly. It suddenly occurred to her that while a little wine was productive of a buoyant happiness, too much might be disastrous. She shook her head, then gasped as a wave of dizziness rolled over her. The old servant's lips twitched. He moved on, discreetly.

From her place at the foot of the table, separated from her daughter's governess only by the masculine bulk of the guest of honor, Pilar was watching her. She was more beautiful than ever in a stiff rose-colored gown, with a jeweled comb in her glossy hair and a heavy gold chain set with emeralds on her magnificent bosom. Her expression, as she turned her head, shocked Daphne out of the alcohol-induced vagueness. Her eyes were narrowed speculatively; she looked from Daphne to Davis and back again even while she leaned in the direction of old Mr. Langley. She was plainly not listening to his rambling monologue.

She's plotting something, the girl thought fearfully. But what? For the first time since she had made her partial confession to Charles, she felt again the panic that had followed each dangerous experience. The open window, the strange tea, the ruined gown.

After all, none of the mysteries had really been explained. Charles' reassurances were as vague as the reasons for her being victimized.

If Pilar were planning mischief, she was its logical object. The kindness shown her in the past few days, Pilar's encouragement of Davis Whitney's suit—these were not directed at pleasing her, but were rather devices by which Pilar was going to get something she wanted for herself.

Charles looked at her inquiringly from the other end of the table. She gave him a bright smile and turned her attention to Mr. Butler, at her right. He said with heavy flattery, "I've been wanting to tell you how charming you look in that flowered frock, Miss Daphne. It's a most becoming fashion for a blooming young lady."

"Thank you." Her smile was mechanical, but he didn't seem to notice. He went on talking. Flattering her, she supposed; Southern gentlemen did seem disposed to compliment ladies whenever they could. It was a pleasant custom, but she didn't hear a word he was saying as she sat with her face turned up to his. She was still aware of Pilar's needle-sharp gaze fixed on the back of her head.

It seemed hours before the hostess finally rose and led the way to the drawing room, the guests following with a clatter of chairs and a rustle of silks. The fine old rug in the drawing room had been covered with tightly stretched crash to make dancing possible; the little piano from the hall stood against a wall, and three tall thin Negroes smiled over the stringed instruments they held. There was a little murmur of pleasure. Old Mrs. Boulanger said happily, "I still like to dance, me." Her small black eyes snapped, "I shall dance with every handsome man here—and I don't see any ugly ones, no, not a one."

Under cover of the laughter that followed Davis whispered to Daphne, "I must dance first with

Mrs. Osborne, since the party is in my honor, and then with Mrs. Boulanger. That is a matter of courtesy, you understand. But I'll be thinking of you every minute and hoping that I may have the next with you."

"Yes, of course."

Seated primly against the wall as the musicians tuned their instruments and then slid into a Strauss waltz, Daphne felt her spirits rise again. She was thankful that she had learned to dance, even though Granny thought it was sinful. Waltzing was wicked, Granny insisted, adding that there was no music prettier than the Blue Danube, just the same. Daphne's white slippers kept time to the haunting strains as couple after couple floated out on the floor, the ladies' skirts billowing softly. She watched Pilar in Davis' arms, her face composed and blank as her body swayed with the music. Charles stepped out gallantly with old Mrs. Boulanger. Mr. Boulanger offered his arm to Isabel, who rose with a smile of pure happiness.

"May I have the honor?"

It was the younger Langley boy, home from college. She rose, smiling.

She still felt a lingering giddiness, but now it merely added to her pleasure as they dipped and whirled to the fairy-like music. The room went around in a whirl of disconnected pictures: walls and windows, paintings and people; Charles' face relaxed and smiling for once; curls tossing, light gleaming on a necklace. Will Langley's arm was snug around her waist. She gave herself up to the magic, moving as lightly as though her slippers trod on air.

She was sorry when the music stopped and her partner returned her to a straight chair near the window. "Thank you, ma'am. I hope you'll favor me again later on."

The musicians struck up again. Davis stood before her, smiling. His teeth were very white, his eyes bright. "Mine, I think?"

"What happened to Mrs. Boulanger?"

"Her husband claimed the honor—quite properly, too."

She followed him into the center of the room. Now that his arm was actually around her, she felt sober and a little frightened.

He said softly, "I've hardly had a chance to speak to you."

She missed a step. "After all, it's your party. Everyone has to welcome the guest of honor."

He bent his head until his lips touched her ear. "It's you I want to see. The others are unimportant."

There was no answer she could make. She gave her attention to the music, which sounded a little scratchy now that she was conscious of it as a separate thing rather than part of an all-encompassing enchantment. Davis danced as well as the Langley boys—she told herself fairly that he did everything well—but there were no longer any rosy clouds under her feet, only a solid floor.

She said regretfully, "I'm afraid I had too much wine at dinner. I feel a little odd."

"Come outside for a minute. The fresh air will make you feel better."

She was sorry she had opened the subject. A private talk with Davis was the last thing she wanted at this point, in her self-conscious confusion. But his hand was under her elbow and he was leading her from the room, through the spacious hall, brightly lighted for the first time since her arrival by candles in the wall sconces. He swung the great front door shut behind them and walked out on the veranda, still holding her arm.

From the house came a diminished sound of music and laughter, less distinct than the chirping of insects in the tall grass and the sleepy complaint of a bird in the treetops.

They were alone in a world flooded with silver-white light, scented with the fragrance of night-blooming flowers. Davis released her arm, but stood so close to her that the scent of fine soap and Virginia cigarettes mingled with the piercing sweetness of honeysuckle. Carefully, as though she were made of porcelain, he put a fingertip under her chin and tipped her head back until she was looking into his eyes.

His face was eager and happy. She closed her eyes.

"Daphne?"

"Yes?"

"I had a speech all prepared, but I seem to have forgotten it. I wasn't going to deliver it until just before leaving Fairlawn, either." He smiled. "I've never told a woman that I loved her. Do I need romantic words—do I have to play Romeo? Not that you don't make a wonderful Juliet, my darling."

She wished that she were far away. *It's a dream,* she thought hopefully. *In a minute I'll wake and get up and have breakfast with Isabel.* She trembled a little as he put his arms around her.

"You know that I love you. You do know, don't you, Daphne?"

She nodded. She had known from the beginning, even before Miguel told her. There was no way she could lie to him, but she wished desperately that she could keep him from going farther.

"Daphne, will you marry me? Will you let me spend the rest of my life making you happy?"

She was afraid to look at him, knowing that all her confusion and reluctance must show in her face.

His kiss took her by surprise. There was no time to turn her face away. For the first time in her life she felt a man's mouth on hers, hot and demanding. Strong arms pressed her against him. She felt the warmth of his body through her thin dress and ruffled petticoats. For a moment she was afraid she was going to faint.

"Tell me you love me, too."

Do I? she wondered. The kiss had startled her, but it had no meaning. She was unable to return it. A stranger's arms encircled her. A friendly and reliable stranger who might become a trusted friend, but no more.

She stepped back. "I can't."

His arms dropped. "Why not? What's the matter, darling? Is it because you need more time,

147

to know me better? I'm sorry if I frightened you by being abrupt."

"I'm sorry, Davis. I like you so much, and you're so good—any woman would be fortunate to win your love. But I can't marry you."

"Are you troubled about my family? My parents will love you, too. They want me to be happy—and they'll welcome you for yourself, darling. In fact, you're exactly the kind of girl they have always wanted me to marry."

She knew that he, too, had thought about the difference in their social position. How could he help it? But it was not the thought of the contrast between her poverty and his wealth that made her hold out a hand to keep him away as he bent to kiss her again. Before her eyes was the image of a face marred by anxiety, the blue-gray eyes questioning.

He asked slowly, "Do you love someone else, Daphne?"

The temptation to lie was almost overwhelming. If she said "yes," and he guessed who the man was—she shivered. Above all things she must keep this impossible, never-to-be-fulfilled love a secret from anyone, locked in the depths of her secret heart. She wanted neither pity nor blame.

But if she let him think she was fancy-free, he would resume his courtship after a tactful interval. She said, still afraid to meet his eyes, "I'm sorry. And honored to know that you care for me. You must believe that."

"A boy back home in Maine?" If his smile was less cheerful than before, it was still an attempt to put her at ease.

She said, in spite of herself, "No."

They looked at each other in silence.

There was a slight creaking sound. Daphne turned sharply. The depths of the hall showed dark against the moon-washed outdoors; she glimpsed a flutter of rose-color as the eavesdropper fled.

"Someone else seeking a breath of air, no doubt," Davis suggested.

The night air was warm, but she felt chilled. She said in a small voice, "We ought to go inside. It's your party. Everyone will be wondering where you are."

They crossed the veranda together, their steps echoing on the marble.

At the door, he put his hand on her arm. His face was pale; there were tears in his eyes. "Let me know if you change your mind. And Daphne, if ever you need a friend, call on me."

She said in a low voice, "Thank you."

She no longer cared whether their absence had been noted and mentioned. She looked from one to another of the women, ignoring their faces, noting in detail the beautiful gowns they wore. Pale yellow, Alice blue, white, emerald green, old Mrs. Boulanger's gauzy black set off by old-fashioned garnets.

Pilar's was the only rose-colored gown in the room. Daphne stared fascinated at the mask-like face above the low bodice, the lips set, the eyes narrow and brooding.

Recalled to the scene by the little stir their reentry caused, she looked around. Her eyes met Daphne's. She turned away quickly, but in that one look all the girl's fears became a blazing certainty. For no reason at all, so far as she knew, Pilar hated her.

XVIII

The candles had burned down to their sockets before the last guests left, with a final exchange of compliments and thanks ringing on the soft night air. Standing with her employers and their guest at the great front door, as the sound of carriage wheels faded away down the drive, Daphne realized that she was tired to the point of exhaustion. The hard work of the past few days, coupled with the nervous excitement of the night's encounter, had left her drained of energy.

She wanted only one thing, to fall into bed without saying another word to anyone and sleep until mind and body were refreshed. Resilient and healthy as she was, the tensions of her life in the past few weeks had been almost too much for her.

She shivered. Davis Whitney, standing beside her, asked solicitously, "Are you cold?"

"No, I'm all right." But it was true that the outdoor air was fresh and a little chilly after the hot rooms and an evening of rich food, wine and dancing. A light breeze had risen and was shaking the heat-wilted leaves.

Charles said, "It's time we were all in bed.

There will be plenty to do tomorrow—today, rather." He added with a strained smile, "Let the lessons go for a few days, Miss Summerfield. I feel very guilty to have added the duties of a housekeeper to your usual tasks. We have taken advantage of your kindness, I'm afraid."

His kind tone and haggard smile were almost more than she could bear, strained and tired as she was. Afraid that she would burst into tears, she managed a watery smile. Both men continued to look at her, their expressions remarkably alike although they were such different types.

A moment, and the spell was broken. She laughed nervously. "I must go in. Good night."

"Good night. I'll look in on Isabel before I retire." For the child, half asleep, had consented to go to bed at midnight. Charles added, "She will sleep all morning, I hope."

Pilar had already gone in, slipping away from the others without a sound as she so often did. There was no sign of her in the downstairs rooms. Daphne glanced nervously into the dining room, which had been cleared of dishes but was still in some disorder; then in the drawing room, where the chairs were still pushed back against the walls, the crumpled crash hid the rug, and a tiny lace-edged handkerchief lay forgotten in the doorway. Tomorrow she would have to supervise the servants as they put everything back into its accustomed stiff pattern.

She was so tired that the thought made her bones and muscles ache, almost as though she herself would have to move all those heavy chairs and tables.

The house was as still as in the days before guests broke its silence. Servants and musicians were long gone, with money and leftover delicacies for their pay. Even Suzanne had retired to her neat little room behind the kitchen. Daphne climbed the stairs slowly and walked as softly as possible past the closed doors that would shelter family and guest this night: the corner guest room prepared for Whitney, Isabel's little pink and white nest, the chamber where Pilar spent so many of her waking as well as her sleeping hours, and the spartan quarters where Charles had lived as a boy. There was no sound from any of them.

It's like an enchanted castle, she thought. *A spell has been laid on it by the wicked witch. But the prince hasn't been able to break it. Will the real prince come disguised as a beggar—or a frog, perhaps?*

Smiling at the childish fancy, she turned the knob of her own bedroom door and found her way confidently into the room, dark as it was. A thin thread of light between the drawn curtains showed that the last rays of the sinking moon still silvered the lawn.

She pulled the heavy fabric apart. The light was pale and gray now, the veranda empty. The two men were perhaps having a nightcap in the dining room or taking a turn around the garden before retiring, as Charles sometimes liked to do.

Closing the curtain, sighing and smiling at the same time, she made her way through the velvety darkness and sank down on the edge of the bed. *Tomorrow,* she thought, *when I am not so tired, I can make some kind of plan for the future.*

The thought was a cheering one. With her rejection of Davis, it became impossible to stay any longer at Fairlawn. It was as though the decision had been made for her.

How many times in these terror-packed weeks had she thought of flight? She had stayed in spite of nameless dangers—ghosts, witches, magic, the evil eye, all the things old Miguel believed in so firmly. Her concern for Isabel, and a natural stubbornness that refused to admit defeat, had kept her at her post. Besides, how could she admit even to herself that she had based so important a decision on the supernatural, when she didn't believe in haunts and spells?

Now she had a sound reason, although she reminded herself nervously that she could never share it with anyone. How could she go on sleeping under the roof that sheltered Charles Osborne, feeling her heart melt at the sight of his tired face across the dinner table, now that she admitted her feelings to herself? Another woman's husband.

Tomorrow, then—

A tiny scrabbling sound broke in on her thoughts. She lifted her head and listened. The rattling of a twig against a glass pane? But there was no tree outside her window.

Something was moving in the room.

She fumbled for matches and a candle. The candlestick was not where she always left it, within easy reach from the bed. She found it and struck a match, the little reddish-yellow circle of its light casting big foolish shadows around chairs and bureau. The candle in her hand, she moved toward the marble-topped washstand where other tapers stood in holders of flowered china.

There was something in the basin. Light in hand, she bent to look. A tan-colored creature with many jointed legs and a long segmented tail moved on the slippery china, making a dry rattling sound as it climbed up a little and slipped back again, finding no foothold.

If she had poured water into the basin in the dark, as she so often did, and washed without lighting a candle, she would have been at the creature's mercy.

She felt the blood drain from her head, and took an instinctive step back, palms pressed against her cheeks. *I must not faint,* she thought urgently, hearing the pounding of her heart.

The nameless danger she had felt around her in the night shadows was here in the room, in the form of a creature no longer than her middle finger—with a sting that could kill.

Since coming to Louisiana, she had learned something of the menace that lies beneath the beauty of that semi-tropical country. Swamps teeming with hungry alligators and the deadly cottonmouth. Mosquitoes whose sting carried malaria. Tiny snakes that looked like strings of coral beads, but were lethal. Things that crept, and bit, and stung.

Death was in her china basin, looking at her out of little evil eyes, struggling to reach her.

An accident? A scorpion could have found its

way into the house through any open door or window, as the big brown spiders did. That one should have reached the second floor and found its way into a basin three feet above floor level seemed unlikely to the point of being ridiculous.

How was she to get rid of the creature? It was senseless to stand here wondering where it had come from; the urgent thing was to destroy it before it could do any harm. It was impossible to drop it out of the window as she did the ugly but harmless spiders—suppose it ran up her arm?

Her first impulse was to flee to Charles for help. She smiled. That would be a fine thing. Knock on his door, rouse Pilar and Davis and have them both come running to see what was the matter?

She found one of the heavy-soled shoes she wore outdoors, and hit at the scorpion. The sound of leather on china was louder than anything she had ever heard. She was afraid, too, of breaking the basin and releasing the thing.

All I need is a poisonous scorpion hidden in my dresser drawers, she thought with a hysterical giggle. She lifted the shoe and swung again. The cracking shell made a sickening sound. Shutting her eyes, she struck a third time and crushed, breaking the bowl down the middle at the same time.

She wrapped a linen towel around bowl and scorpion both, so that she wouldn't have to look at them in the morning. She thought, *I'll show it to Charles tomorrow*. And remembered, for the first time, that Davis Whitney was staying until

Friday, and she would have no chance to speak to Charles privately until after he left.

That brought up the question of her behavior toward Davis. Every encounter would be an embarrassment to both of them; every look he directed at her, a reproach.

It's all my fault, she thought. *He is kind and good, a man who deserves the best of everything. And yet, how can I spend my life with a man I don't love—worst of all, while thoughts of another, forever beyond my reach, torment my days and disturb my nights?*

In any case, she had given him her decision and it was final. He was not a man to beg, once having been rebuffed.

She undressed quickly and got into bed, arranging the mosquito net with great care because she couldn't help imagining an army of fanged, biting and stinging creatures converging on her in her sleep. She knew that she was being foolish, but she felt safer once she was within the shelter of the thin white curtain.

Even so, she lay awake for a long time. She heard the two men come up the stairs together, separate with a murmured "good night" and go to their respective rooms. Again and again, she tried to plan for the next day, and found herself without an answer. The first rays of the morning sun were creeping in between the curtains before she fell into a broken sleep, burdened with frightful dreams and interrupted by startled wakings.

XIX

When she awoke, the hands of the little traveling clock on the bedside table pointed to ten-fifteen. She lay still for a moment, collecting her thoughts, puzzled by the feeling of apprehension and nervous fear that crept over her as consciousness returned. Something dreadful had happened—but what?

A little dizzy with sleeplessness and tension, she sat up in bed and looked around the room. At the sight of the towel-swaddled basin, memory came flooding back. The scorpion, last in a series of strange misadventures. Something in this house was trying to destroy her. Whether it was something supernatural, as Miguel so firmly believed, or human hatred, she was in grave danger.

I must get away from this place, she thought *—now, today.* She recalled reading a romance by Edgar Allan Poe in which the helpless victim saw the walls closing in on him, pushing him toward a horrible pit that yawned beneath his feet. Reading the story in her snug little room at home, it had been merely entertaining. Now it seemed to her that she, too, was being pushed to her own destruction as surely as though the walls of Fair-lawn were closing in around her.

But why? Why should anyone want to destroy her, when she never had done anyone harm?

It was impossible to stay in bed any longer,

tired though she was after her almost sleepless night. She got up and, avoiding the broken basin with its ghastly but now harmless contents, pulled on her clothes with shaking hands. As she buttoned the collar of her blouse, her hands touched the little gold locket, the only ornament her mother had left her. In the panic of the previous evening, she had forgotten to take it off.

Sick at heart, she realized that her ordeal was not yet over. Her half-formed plans for an immediate departure could not be carried out as long as Davis Whitney was on the premises. It would be easy enough to go to Charles, tell him of this latest development and ask him for transportation to the railway depot. During one of her wakeful hours it had even occurred to her that Miguel, appealed to, would spirit her away without the formality of saying goodbye to her employers. The old man was her firm friend, and she could explain everything in a letter, from a safe distance.

She was no coward, but she flinched from the thought of facing Pilar's scorn, and her heart ached at the prospect of saying goodbye to Isabel. The child had become very dear to her. As for taking leave of Isabel's father, knowing that she would never see him again—

Now she realized that it was impossible. Davis was a guest in the house, before whom appearances must be kept up. He would understand her reasons for leaving, would help her if she threw herself on his mercy; even though she had rejected him as a suitor, she knew that she could depend upon his chivalry. If she had been thinking only of herself, she would have fled to him for help in this moment of tension.

But there was another thing to consider. He was Charles' friend, and his business associate as well. All of Charles' hopes of rebuilding the Osborne fortune and restoring Fairlawn to its early splendor depended upon him. He would be shocked or curious, or worst of all, pitying. For all his Creole heritage, she doubted whether he really believed in ghosts and witches. And once an outsider knew about the strange goings-on at Fairlawn, they would become public property. There would be gossip, rumors, perhaps an investigation.

She could not do that to Charles, and eventually to Isabel. It would have to be Miguel and the clandestine departure, after all.

Having made her decision, she was ready to act on it. Her little round-topped trunk was stored in the attic. There was no way to get it without attracting attention. Very well, she would leave most of her belongings here. They were of no great value anyway. She got her valise down from the shelf of the wardrobe and began packing the few things that she treasured most; her grandmother's shabby Bible, a few sturdy garments, and the little stacks of bills and gold pieces that Charles, hard pressed for ready money as he was, had put into her hand on the first day of every month. With Granny's practicality, she counted her little hoard before putting it into the bottom of the satchel. There would be enough to keep her until she found employment.

On impulse, she decided to take the flowered lawn she had worn the night before. *A souvenir of high society,* she thought with a touch of her grandmother's irony. She turned to the chair where she had hastily thrown her clothes after killing the scorpion.

The flowered lawn, slashed from neck to hem, fell apart in her hands.

She pressed her palm against her mouth to hold back a scream.

Granny's tart voice sounded in her ears, as though her thoughts of the old lady had summoned up that protective spirit. *"Go for help. This is no time to be squeamish."*

With new determination, she threw open her bedroom door. It was standing ajar, a half-inch of light showing through the crack.

She remembered the satisfying click of the latch the night before. Someone had opened her door while she slept, taking infinite care not to rouse her. Someone had come into her room again, bent on destruction—perhaps to gloat over her lifeless body, if the scorpion had done its work. It was no ghost. Ghosts don't carry scissors, she thought wryly, examining the cut edges of the destroyed garment.

Clutching the remnants of the flowered dress, she ran through the silent hall and down the wide staircase, not caring now what scandal she started or what questions she aroused. The stairs were splashed with sunlight from the landing window. She did not see it. She was not sure what she would do when she saw Charles—cry, scream, go into peals of hysterical laughter. All three seemed possible.

She was sure of one thing: even if Davis Whitney were present, she was going to put as much distance as possible between Fairlawn and herself before darkness fell again.

There was no one in the downstairs rooms. The two Negro women who were supposed to come back and put the rooms in order had apparently not arrived, and the salon was just as she had left it, even to the little fragile handkerchief dropped and forgotten on the threshold. She burst into the morning room, where a clutter of plates and cups suggested that at least two persons had breakfasted, and into the kitchen where Suzanne was patiently washing the crystal wine glasses.

"Suzanne, where is Mr. Osborne?"

The old woman waved a hand vaguely toward the back door.

"In the fields, with a guest?"

Suzanne shook her head, her dark face expressing a strong desire to say something. Daphne thought, as so often before, how much patience and faith she must have to bear the frustration of speechlessness.

"In the stables? Thank you."

Still clutching the ruined dress to her bosom, she ran across the back yard and pushed open the door of the stable. It was cool and shadowy inside, and she looked around hopefully. *Miguel is my friend,* she reminded herself. *He will get me out of this place.*

But Miguel was nowhere in sight. Charles sat on his blanket-covered cot, deep in thought. At the sound of footsteps he lifted his head. She was shocked at his weary and hopeless expression. "Daphne! What has happened?"

She held out the shredded dress. "Someone came in my room while I was asleep. The door had been opened. Charles, I'm frightened. Someone here hates me." She looked at him for reassurance, but his face had gone dead white; his eyes reflected her terror. "There was a poison scorpion in my basin last night. Luckily I heard it move and lit the candle—whoever put it there knew that I often undress in the dark—"

"You're not hurt!"

"No, I killed it. I can't stay here any longer, Charles. Too many things have happened."

He said slowly, "I'm afraid that you are right. I had hoped that I could protect you, but now I see that it's impossible. Miguel will take you to the afternoon train." He smiled slightly. "He isn't here just now—he has accompanied Mr. Whitney to his relatives' plantation, where they will leave his borrowed rig, and then he'll drive him to Fairlawn Station. They ought to be arriving now." He smiled again. "All these departures are keeping the poor old man on the run."

"Mr. Whitney has left?"

"Called away by urgent business, so he says." Charles looked at her intently. "I take it you refused his proposal of matrimony. Or was it something else that he proposed?"

"Oh, no, he wanted to marry me." She was silent for a moment, reliving that impetuous proposal on the veranda. "I don't feel about him as a woman ought to feel towards the man she marries. I'm sorry, but I can't help it."

"Daphne." His voice went flat. "No, never mind. Do you want to say goodbye to Isabel? She's going to miss you."

She shook her head, unable to speak. The concern in his voice was suddenly more than she could bear, added to the terror of the night and the strain of the past weeks. Tears rose to her eyes and spilled down her cheeks. She turned her head away.

Osborne said helplessly, "Don't." He jumped up and stood beside her. "Daphne, darling." His arms closed around her. The scraps of flowered lawn fell unnoticed to the floor. She laid her head against his shoulder and sobbed, comforted by his nearness. And more than comforted. There was a dangerous sweetness in his touch, an excitement and wonder that she had missed in Davis' embrace, even without knowing what it was that was lacking.

The silence that bound them was broken by the sound of light footsteps and the creaking of the stable door.

Charles' arms dropped. Daphne took a step backward. Both of them turned to the doorway of Miguel's little room. But whoever had entered the stable was gone, silently.

Charles said harshly, "Don't tell anyone you are going. Not anyone, do you understand? I'll see Miguel when he returns. And Daphne—"

He hesitated. "I have to go to Saint Laurent," he said. "I have business with the law. I'll not be here for lunch. But I want to see you again before you leave. There's something I must explain to you."

XX

The day seemed endless. She was glad when Isabel came in from her morning ride, flushed and full of cheerful chatter about the party. "When I grow up I'm going to marry a man with a big plantation, and we'll give dinner parties all the time. Big ones like the dinners my grandmother used to give at Fairlawn—the first Fairlawn." She sighed rapturously. "Forty people at the table, and French wine, and waiters in livery. I can hardly wait."

"You had better learn the nine tables first," Daphne said, with a smile to take the sting out of her words. She would miss this loving child. And what would happen to Isabel, left behind with a mother who seemed completely indifferent to her existence and a father always overburdened with work and worry?

She said with an effort, "It's nearly one o'clock. Let's go and see what Suzanne has for lunch."

"Mr. Whitney went away; did you know that?" Isabel held the heavy front door open for her. "I like him a lot; don't you? He likes you, too."

Daphne's smile was strained. "Yes, of course, but let's not talk about him."

"But do you like him?"

"Yes, of course I do."

The dining room was still in disorder, the table draped with rumpled and wine-stained linen. Isabel beamed. "My mother isn't coming down to lunch. She never does when she has been up late the night before. You know, when Tio Felipe lived here we had lots of parties—well, not lots," she corrected herself, "but some. That was fun."

"Your uncle lived here, at Fairlawn?"

"Of course. Half of the plantation was his. My mother didn't like him," Isabel explained, "and he didn't like her either. But half of Fairlawn belonged to him because he and my papa were twins. He was the one who wanted to plant rice. Now it all belongs to my father and it will be mine someday, because Tio Felipe died in Spain." Her face clouded. "I wish he hadn't. I'd rather have him than Fairlawn."

Daphne felt that she was under enough strain without all this talk of death and inheritances. She was relieved to find that Suzanne had set the table for two in the sunny little morning room, even though she had no appetite and could only push the food around on her plate. Isabel ate with her usual zest. "Being out in the fresh air makes me hungry and sleepy," she said with a yawn, "but more hungry. Maybe I'll take a siesta, like a grown-up lady. After all, I didn't go to bed till after midnight!"

"That's a good idea." *Then I can leave without farewells or explanations,* Daphne thought thankfully. Drained of emotion and facing an unknown future which at the moment seemed to hold very little promise, she wanted nothing except to get away. Even the thought of a last meeting with Charles was painful. What could they say that would not wound both of them?

But her heart leaped when, on mounting the stairs to her room, she found a small folded paper tucked under her pin tray. She read it twice. *"I will be waiting for you on Hidden Island this afternoon. Young Pierre Loizeau will meet you behind the stable at three o'clock, to escort you there. If you care for me, do not fail me. C."*

She was still afraid of the gray-green swamps with their overhanging trees and the hidden life multiplying below the surface of the water. Why had he chosen the island for their last meeting? True, it had been his childhood refuge, but that scarcely seemed a good reason for bringing her there—merely to say goodbye.

Never mind, she thought defiantly, knowing that she would do whatever he asked her to.

Not until she was riding through the deepening gloom of the woods, with the silent and shifty-eyed Loizeau boy alongside on a farm nag, did she realize that the rendezvous would keep her from catching the afternoon train at Fairlawn Station.

She assured herself that Charles must have made some other plan for her. Perhaps he would take her to Saint Laurent and put her in the care of kind Mrs. Jackson. Perhaps there was an evening train that the master of Fairlawn could flag to a stop. At any rate, she trusted him.

She recalled her earlier fears, and tried to dismiss them, but she couldn't help reflecting that she had no proof of his innocence, even now. Was she riding into a trap?

She glanced uneasily at the Loizeau boy. He had not said a word since they started. Of course, he spoke only Cajun. So far as holding a conversation was concerned, she would have been better off with Suzanne—this young lout could not understand her, either, and his face was blank. There was no way to make him turn back, and she did not know the way through this dark and frightening place. She had no choice but to follow him.

They rode on, into the deepening gloom of the old trees with their ghostly wreaths of gray moss.

XXI

The journey began to seem endless. Daphne reminded herself that it had been long on the day of the picnic, too; and then she had been riding in a well-built buggy, not on the back of a horse. Bluebird was docile, but she had ridden only a few times before and still gasped in panic when her mount stumbled over a root or splashed through a puddle. *I'll be stiff when this is over*, she thought gloomily—*if it ever is.*

Pierre Loizeau led the way on his swaybacked bay without glancing back to see if she was following. She had heard a great deal about the Cajuns, their jovial good nature, their love of music and wine, their free and easy hospitality. Apparently this youth was an exception. Once, he glanced around; she managed to smile, but he quickly turned away and rode on.

They entered a stretch of forest so dense that sunlight could not filter through the branches. The air was cool and still, as though no breath of wind had ever entered, and no bird sang.

She was glad when they reached the rim of the water, where a smaller version of the Loizeau boy greeted his brother with a brief phrase in patois and led away both the horses. A small pirogue lay half in the water, half on the marshy shore. The Loizeau boy motioned her to get in, pushed the pirogue away from land and poled out into the stream before she was well seated.

She reminded herself that she would come back with Charles, and tried not to look at the water that rose so close to the top of the boat or the hummocks that rose here and there, some with good-sized trees growing on them. On the opposite shore a shell ridge made a long narrow crest against the sky. A long-legged bird stalked along the edge, uttering weird high-pitched cries. She shivered. Would she ever be in the land of safe familiar things, where wrens and robins built their nests?

She wondered how anyone could find his way through these unmarked water lanes without getting lost, but Pierre seemed to know what he was doing. She remembered that Davis had said there were men who knew these bayous like their back yards, men who could pole a pirogue two hundred miles or more and never miss a turning.

If he would only do something! she thought, eying the sullen-looking back of the Loizeau boy's head. Talk, or sing, or even shake his fist! She giggled. He turned and looked at her, but his expression did not change and after a brief scrutiny he turned away again and gave all his attention to piloting their tipping craft.

By the time he landed the vessel, she was tired and headachy. She managed to scramble onto land and pick her way along the squashy shore, keeping a sharp eye out for snakes, turtles and unknown creatures that might be hiding in the grass. It was not until she reached a dry spot and stopped to catch her breath that she realized the Loizeau boy was not behind her. He was in the boat, pulling away out of sight around a bend. She stood looking after him, feeling really alarmed now that she was alone.

She looked around for a landmark, anything that she could recognize from her first trip to the island. Neither the fallen logs where they had sat to eat nor the hollow-tree postoffice about which Pilar had lost her temper were to be seen. She was in a strange place!

Of course, she thought, *it's only that we landed farther downstream—if this sluggish water can be called a stream. And I wasn't looking for landmarks that time.* She remembered Isabel, urged by her father to take an interest in botany, saying that it was all she could do to tell the difference between a live oak and a water oak, let alone care what kind of cells made them. She laughed shakily. The sound was strange on the silent air.

Charles was nowhere in sight. She supposed,

sensibly, that he had been delayed. She fought down an urge to walk along the shore looking for him. What if he came and found her gone?

She sat down on a dry tussock and waited. Her head was aching badly now, and a hollow feeling reminded her that she had missed both breakfast and lunch, and the afternoon was well along. At that moment she would have welcomed the sound of any human voice, the sight of any face—even Jean Lafitte's, she thought whimsically. The setting really called for a blackbrowed, swarthy pirate in gold earrings.

There was a splashy sound which even her inexperienced ear recognized as a pirogue being beached; then a rustling of grass and twigs as someone came near. She jumped up. "Charles!"

The sounds became louder. She stood with a hand at her throat, waiting.

Pilar appeared from behind a large tree, picking her way daintily around the wet spots in small high-heeled slippers.

XXII

The color drained from Daphne's face, leaving it bone-white. She stood as though rooted to the spot. Pilar smiled, and it was not a pleasant smile. "Are you expecting someone?" she asked coldly.

"Did—did Charles send you?"

"You might say so." Pilar's voice was calm, as

always. "I came to look for a ring I lost the last time I was here. Come on; help me find it."

I don't want to go anywhere with this woman, Daphne thought. She would have screamed if anyone had been within earshot; even the silent company of the Loizeau boy was preferable to the undefined menace in Pilar's tone. Yet the woman seemed friendly enough; and how could she refuse to accompany her, without explaining that she was here to meet a man—none other than Pilar's own husband?

They walked along together, Daphne now and then stumbling over a hidden root or a tuft of weeds and grasses. Pilar, for all her dizzy heels, moved as smoothly as a swan in midstream. Daphne remembered that Pilar had been a barefoot child in this wild and treacherous country, that it was as familiar to her as the rocky beaches of Maine to a girl brought up on the Atlantic.

She said in a small, brave attempt at making conversation, "I've been wondering—that is, I didn't recognize the place where we landed. Of course, I'm not very good at outdoor things, but I did remember the big oaks and the fallen trees where we ate, the other time."

Pilar said something in a low voice. Daphne thought it was, "It's not the same," but she couldn't be sure. She was silent.

They had been walking for several minutes before she realized that instead of following the shoreline, they were going deeper inland. She stopped. "Is the picnic ground on the other side of the island?"

Pilar halted, too. For a moment they stood

looking at each other, Pilar's face mocking, Daphne's questioning. "No. We are not on Hidden Island."

"We—what!"

"This is not Hidden Island. Nobody would ever come here for a picnic," Pilar said, as though she were explaining an obvious fact to a backward child. "This is Dead Man's Island."

A chill seized Daphne. It was all she could do to keep her knees from shaking. Pilar asked softly, "Do you know why they call it that?"

Daphne ran her tongue over dry lips. "No."

Pilar's laugh had the hard ring of metal. It was more frightening than a curse would have been. "You'll find out. If I were you, I wouldn't be in any hurry to get where we are going."

"What do you mean?"

"Never mind. Come along." She walked on rapidly, and Daphne followed reluctantly, wishing with all her heart that she had not come here in the first place. She could not have said which she feared more, the solitude of the lonely island or the other woman's menacing presence. *Maybe*, she thought desperately, *it's a joke. Maybe Charles will be waiting for us on the other shore, or Miguel, and we'll go back to Fairlawn together.*

Or maybe—she felt a new rise of hope—Pilar had not known that she was meeting Charles here, and he would appear in time to save her from whatever unknown terror awaited her.

But she felt sure that this was all Pilar's doing, and that they were alone on—she shivered—Dead Man's Island. She looked around fearfully, as though a bleached skeleton might be lying under any tree. "Where are we going?"

"Oh, this will be far enough. No one can see us from the shore. Not that anyone is there to see."

"I don't understand. What do you mean?"

For the second time, Pilar turned to face her. This time she was really smiling. At the sight of those thin lips pulled back over sharp white teeth, Daphne took a nervous step backward, suppressing a strong desire to scream.

"This is what I mean," Pilar said in a low ice-cold voice, the smile vanishing. "You can't have my husband."

She laughed at the look that flashed over the girl's face. "You stupid, pasty-faced, sneaky little idiot! Did you think for one moment that the two of you had me fooled? I've been watching you since the night you first came to Fairlawn. I've seen you plotting to steal Carlos from me, smiling at him, making excuses to win his pity, stealing away to be alone with him, looking at him with those big blue eyes—"

She's insane, Daphne thought. Not angry and jealous, but utterly mad. Reason would never get through to her, and she was incapable of pity even when rational. Panic set her teeth to chattering. She was trapped on a deserted island, alone with a madwoman who hated her!

Pilar's face was white, her eyes like hot coals. She took a step forward, her hand raised. Daphne shrank back. "Since the day he came back from Spain he has never embraced me, never knocked at my door. He has changed to me and to everyone. I could have changed him back if you had accepted the Whitney boy and gone away from Fairlawn—he would have come back to me!"

Her face was a tragic mask. Frightened as she was, the girl felt a pang of sympathy. Dangerous or not, Pilar was suffering, had suffered longer than anyone knew beneath that cool composure.

Like a knife came the realization that Pilar was going to make her suffer, too. If the open window and ruined dresses had been merely attempts to get her out of the way, the failure of Davis' courtship had made Pilar determined to do away with her. She had passed beyond suspicion to a hatred as deadly and impersonal as that of a housewife who kills a poisonous insect —as grim as Daphne's own determination to destroy the scorpion.

Pilar's voice rose to a demented shriek. "Do you think I don't know why you refused Davis Whitney? That I don't know Carlos comes to you in the night? Why he stays in that little room at the end of the hall, while I lie awake and wait for him? I know—I've watched both of you. You've put a spell on him with your baby face and those silly simpering ways. But when you're gone, Carlos will come back to me."

It was useless to protest her innocence. She said hopefully, "Look, I'm leaving Fairlawn this afternoon, right away. I'm never coming back. Everything will be all right."

"You're never coming back to Fairlawn," Pilar agreed. Her eyes glittered. She took another step toward Daphne. "You will never steal another married man. Why do you think I wrote that note?"

"*You* wrote it?"

"Of course. Were you fool enough to believe that Carlos would leave a letter where anyone could find it?" Pilar's laugh was scornful. "I told you that you were a fool. You came here to meet him. I was afraid you might not—it was the only thing I feared."

Daphne said, trying to keep her voice calm, "All right. Let's go back to Fairlawn now. I'll leave at once if you want me to."

Pilar shook her head. "You will never leave this island. Your bones will lie with those of the men who died here in the old days, when the pirates brought their enemies to this place." She laughed mockingly as Daphne looked around. "Oh, you'll not find their bodies! They lie at the bottom of the quicksand—if it has a bottom. There are those who think that it reaches down to hell."

"Please."

"You can't escape it. And if you do," Pilar said with a dreadful smile, "you'll die of hunger and thirst. That hurts, too."

Daphne said with spirit, "Charles will look for me."

"Oh, no. You have already left Fairlawn. The Boulangers' coachman took you to Fairlawn Station after lunch. You left a very proper note addressed to Carlos and me." She laughed. "I haven't opened it. I am leaving that pleasure to him."

"The Loizeau boy—"

"Will say nothing. He is afraid of me." She added, "It was thoughtful of you to pack your valise. It's at the bottom of the bayou."

Daphne said slowly, "It was you who cut up the dresses, and put the poison in my tea. You wanted to kill me."

"I wanted to plunge the scissors into your heart, and watch the blood flow!" Pilar said. "At first I only wanted to frighten you, but you got away from me. You won't get away this time." She smiled craftily. "And Charles will never know, so he can love me again."

They faced each other, hunter and hunted.

Pilar broke first. "I'll torture you first!" she shouted. "I'll tear you to pieces—I'll dig your eyes out with my nails and leave them for the vultures!" She sprang at Daphne, hands reaching for her throat.

For a horrible moment the girl seemed rooted to the spot. It was like the nightmares of her childhood, with her feet held fast in a morass while a ravening monster rushed at her. Using all her will, she forced herself to take a step. The spell was broken. She began to run.

She had little hope of eluding the sure-footed Pilar, who seemed tireless in her insane anger; and where would she go, cut off from the mainland by the murky waters of the bayou? She felt a hope, a slight hope, but enough to lend speed to her feet. If she could reach the water's edge and follow it until she reached Pilar's pirogue—if she could push off from the shore before those talon-like fingers closed around her throat—she had a chance.

Dodging, tripping over roots, saved from falling only because she was young and desperate, she ran in the direction from which they had come. Against the murderous gleam in her pursuer's eyes, a fragile shell bobbing on the infested waters of the bayou was refuge and salvation.

She had forgotten how spongy this ground was, how mud and water oozed up from solid-looking earth under the weight of a human being. Moisture seeped around her soles, crept up the sides of her shoes. She struggled on toward a rise in the ground. The mud pulled her back. She jerked one foot loose, then the other, only to realize that she was imbedded almost ankle-deep.

It was her nightmare come true, and worse, because there would be no waking in the dear safety of her own room. This was real and final.

A burst of manic laughter startled her. Half-turning, she looked back. Pilar had abandoned the chase. She stood a few feet away, leaning against a small tree, her face twisted in laughter. "Run you fool!"

Quicksand, Daphne thought. She pulled a foot loose and took another step only to find herself trapped again.

There was a little knoll not more than six feet away. If she could get to it, she would be safe. She took a long step, topped forward on her hands and knees, and jerked herself upright in growing terror. Pilar, watching, was motionless. Once more Daphne was reminded of the narrow-eyed motionless cat waiting for its victim.

She made a last attempt to cajole her captor. "All right, it's a good joke. Now help me get out, and we'll go back."

"Do you think I'm crazy? If I let you go, you'll try to steal my husband again."

Now it was not only water but mud that oozed over the tops of her shoes, wetting her ankles and smearing her stockings. It was innocent-looking stuff, but it gripped and held like a vise. She took another step and then another, sinking deeper with each one.

"Die, you fool!" Pilar stooped to pick up something, hurled it with all her strength. Daphne doubled. The stone whizzed past her head, but now the sucking mud was calf high and it took all her strength to pull a foot free. She cried in an anguish of fear, "Pilar!"

But Pilar was off, crashing through trees and shrubs like a fleeing deer. She had kicked off her shoes. They lay in the grass like little deserted animals, and she ran like her gypsy mother.

She would go back to Fairlawn, Daphne thought dully, and take up the life she had led before the governess appeared to trigger her hatred: an indolent, aimless life, spending long hours in her room, taking no interest in the management of her house. If Isabel complained that Miss Summerfield never wrote, her mother would offer no comment. And no one would ever know what had happened.

In a way, that was the worst.

She tried to pray for courage, but her mind would not shape the words. It would be a horrible death, she thought sickly as she struggled anew to free her feet from the sticky mass. This time it took all her strength to get the left foot out, and her shoe stayed behind.

Like drowning, but slower; a gradual smothering as the quicksand crept into her nose and throat, as she struggled in vain to hold her face above the smothering stuff, as her breathing grew harder and her head sank below the surface. Held in that remorseless embrace, she would be lost from sight forever.

She took a deep breath and screamed at the top of her voice, "Help! Help!"

The answer was silence.

Keep moving, she ordered herself. The dampness was creeping higher, slowly but remorselessly. This time it took all her strength to wrench a foot free, and it seemed to her that the other sank deeper as she rested her whole weight on it.

She fixed her eyes on the little hill. Five or six short steps, and she would be safe. She brushed away the chilling realization that she would still be trapped on the island, even if she gained that temporary refuge. Even if she escaped the quicksand in her search for the shore, there was no way to get back to the mainland. But it would be better to starve, better to drink the slimy bayou water than to undergo the torture of suffocation.

She struggled to pull her leg free, but the more she struggled the faster she seemed to be sinking.

I'm going to die, she thought. But she went on with grim determination, fighting to free herself from the morass.

When she lifted one leg, the other was pulled down further. Panicked, she gathered all her strength and screamed again. She was not sure how far inland Pilar had led her, but if fishermen or hunters were passing, and if they heard her, there was a one-in-a-million chance that they would reach her in time.

Only silence answered her.

A light breeze stirred the leaves and grasses, and lifted the hair from her perspiring forehead.

Suddenly, with absolute certainty, she remembered reading that if she tried to move, she would sink even faster. Her only hope was to remain absolutely still, and pray that someone would be passing who might hear her cries.

As terrifying as this knowledge was, she forced herself to stay motionless, using her last dregs of strength to cry out sporadically in the ever-darkening twilight. . . .

The world had dwindled to a few square feet of greedy earth, sucking her down slowly but inevitably into horror and final oblivion.

Tentatively she would try to move toward that high knoll again, only to recognize that each movement pulled her further down, down to that horrible—

No, I mustn't think of that, she said to herself. *I must concentrate on breathing, staying still and hope for rescue.* Rescue—even as she thought of it, she knew that only a miracle would bring someone to this desolate spot.

It seemed as if hours of dreadful eternity had passed when she heard sounds in the direction of the shore. *Pilar*, she thought, coming back, after all, to rescue her.

Or to gloat over her final agony?

She screamed again. "Help! Help me!"

Charles Osborne came into sight, with the two Loizeau boys at his heels. His face was dead white and he carried a coil of rope.

Trees and sky began to go around in slow, sickening circles. Sparks exploded before her eyes and she ceased to exist.

XXIII

"Daphne. Darling Daphne, I'll never let you go again."

Daphne opened her eyes. She was lying on the little grassy hill she had struggled in vain to reach—or was that all a bad dream? She felt that it had happened hundreds and hundreds of years ago, in some almost-forgotten other life.

It didn't matter. Charles' arms were around her, and her head was cradled on his shoulder. She sighed contentedly.

"Here, don't go back to sleep! I have to know what happened. It was Pilar, wasn't it?"

"You wrote a note." She opened her eyes, trying to focus them on his face. "She wrote it, of course."

"Wrote me one, too. She's always been able

to imitate other people's handwriting—voices, too. What I can't understand is why you came here with her. You must have known she was the one who tried to harm you before."

"You said you wanted to see me before I went away. The boy came after me—I thought he was acting on your orders."

"You'd do that for me, afraid of the swamp as you are?"

She nodded, burying her face against the front of his shirt so that he might not see the love in her eyes. "I still don't understand. How did you know where to find me?"

His laugh was grim. "I found the note you thought I'd written on your bureau, when I got back from Saint Laurent—I'd gone there on some legal business that will change the whole picture at Fairlawn, by the way. I knew right away what had happened, of course. She was in that room of hers with the door locked—good God, how much evil she's plotted in that room! I broke the door down," Charles said grimly, "and she told me the whole thing. She'd have killed me, I think, if she could have got her hands on a gun or a knife."

Daphne shuddered. A raving madwoman shut up in the old plantation house, boiling with hate for everyone—it was a frightening picture. A new fear struck at her. She pulled herself up to a sitting position, ignoring the aches and twinges that stirred when she moved. "Isabel?"

"In the stable with Miguel and Suzanne. Miguel will guard her with his life, if he has to." He pulled her back into the shelter of his arms.

"Once I got my hands on Pierre Loizeau, the rest was easy. Pilar had him scared into believing that she had supernatural powers and would put a curse on him if he told—Miguel's not the only one in these parts who believes in witches! But his father got the story out of him. Don Jaime saved his life once, and the Cajuns don't forget a debt of gratitude."

"Oh, God, if you hadn't come! Even if I never see you again," Daphne said simply, "I've had this—this coming back to life in your arms, and knowing that you care for me. I'll remember it as long as I live."

"What do you mean, never see me again?" His arms tightened around her. "We're going to be married. Unless you prefer young Whitney, of course. He has a good deal more to offer—money, and social position, and a house on Prytania Street."

"But, Charles!"

"No. Charles is buried in the mountains of Andalusia."

She pulled herself away and looked wonderingly into his face. It was strained with anxiety and daubed with mud, but what she saw there reassured her. She said slowly, "You're Philip, of course. Why didn't I see—why couldn't I understand? But she didn't know either. She thought you were the other one. That you stopped acting like a husband because—oh, dear!"

"You ought to blush more often. It's quite becoming, even through a heavy layer of swamp mud."

"But she said—"

"I always hated her," he said angrily. "She trapped my brother into marriage before he was old enough to understand what was happening, or to care that she was a liar and thief and a screaming virago when anyone crossed her. She ignored Isabel from the day of her birth." He looked searchingly at Daphne. "I love that child. She can live with us, can't she? I don't think there will be any trouble about the legal aspects of it, once Pilar is in the asylum where she belongs."

Daphne nodded, but she hardly heard him. Her mind was traveling with lightning speed over the happenings of the last few weeks, gathering bits of the puzzle and fitting them together. "It was Charles who died in the train wreck."

"Of course. I switched the papers."

"But why?"

"Charles was a coward and a weakling. I loved him; we were close as only twins can be, but I knew his faults. He meant well, but he was lazy and careless. That woman sapped his will. What we accomplished at Fairlawn was my doing. I had to push and prod him every step of the way."

He put a finger under Daphne's chin and tipped her head back until their eyes met. "Don't you see? If Philip had come home, Pilar would have inherited two-thirds of the plantation: a third as Charles' widow and a third as Isabel's guardian. She would have run me off the place. The estate would have fallen deeper and deeper into ruin. And Isabel, alone with that woman, no one to act as a parent toward her—"

"Miguel knew all the time."

"I think so. He never spoke of it."

"You did the right thing." She had almost forgotten where they were. Even the horror of the afternoon seemed far away and unimportant in the light of these astounding revelations. "But how will you prove that you're Philip? Everyone will think you've gone mad, too."

He shouted with laughter. "Darling, I already have a notarized statement from André Perron, and two deputy sheriffs waiting for us at the boundary of Fairlawn. André and the circuit judge and the state representative from this parish are my friends from boyhood. So is the priest at Saint Jean Baptiste, for that matter. They've gone swimming with me many times. There's a long scar on my thigh from a day when I nearly drowned—and a birthmark which I shall not describe." He chuckled. "There, you're blushing again."

"No, I'm not." She looked around, still leaning against him for strength and comfort. "Charles. Philip, I mean. How are we going to get out of this place?"

"My good girl, I know every inch of Dead Man's Island. All of us did. Pilar had no trouble avoiding the quicksand, you'll remember. You can follow my footsteps out. Or I'll carry you, if you prefer."

"I can walk." But it was all she could do to struggle to her feet; her back and legs hurt almost unbearably and her head swam. "I do feel odd, but I don't mind a bit," she assured him.

"How do we get away from this horrible island, then?"

"Oh, the Loizeaus are waiting for us with two pirogues and a store of gossip that will keep every household from here to Grand Ile buzzing for months. I must warn you that you reputation will be in shreds by this time tomorrow. After all, we've been alone all this time without a chaperone. I may have to marry you to make an honest woman of you."

She felt the color rising in her cheeks. "I may accept you if you propose properly, but I am not going to become engaged until I have a chance to wash my face."

He took her hand. "It won't be easy. Pilar will fight, even with two armed deputies to take her. There will be certain legal forms to go through before I can establish my identity. Will you wait for me?"

She slipped her hand into his. "I'll wait for you the rest of my life. We're never going to be separated again."

XXIV

The southern dusk had changed to night as a party of four turned in at the stone gateposts: Daphne and Philip on his gray saddle horse, her arms around his waist for support and assurance; and two deputies on their official mounts. The men's faces were set and stern. The Loizeau boys had been dismissed at the water's edge with thanks and promises of rewards to come. Philip, at least, had no trouble talking to them.

"Philip, be careful. I'm afraid."

"I'll take care of you, darling."

It was for his safety she feared, but she closed her lips tightly over the admission. He turned his head to look at her as the three horses came abreast in the long lane, and his expression was an unspoken caress. "By this time tomorrow the worst will be over," he said gently. "Keep that in mind."

"I will."

The older of the deputies saluted. "You want the lady should stay here while we go up to the house and investigate, sir? It might be safer if there's any violence."

Daphne said clearly, "I am staying with you."

"We may not have any trouble," Philip said slowly. "All right, stay behind me, then, no matter what happens."

The three horses advanced slowly, side by side, their hoofbeats muffled in the soft dust.

Daphne looked at the sober faces of the men, and tightened her hold on Philip. The prayer that had been denied to her in her own moment of peril rose to her lips. Nothing mattered except his safety, neither her own peril nor Pilar's lust for vengeance.

The plantation house stood dark and silent, it's white pillars gleaming. Farther back and to one side a square of dull yellow light showed where Miguel's lantern burned. She thought of Isabel and the two faithful servants in that humble shelter, barricaded against danger like the early settlers in their log cabins, and fear for them stabbed her. If Pilar had revenged herself on them, it might be too late.

Never had the countryside seemed so desolate or so remote. She felt a homesick pang for the little Maine village with friendly lamplight outlining the windows, and familiar faces at every garden gate. Would this sparsely-settled country ever seem like home to her?

The answer came quick and clear. Home was wherever Philip was.

The younger deputy asked in a hoarse whisper, "What will we do if she's left?"

"She hasn't. But if she has, we'll organize the neighbors and call out the law from here to Saint Jean Baptiste. I won't have my fiancée or my niece in any more danger—and while that woman is at large, no one is safe."

The others nodded slowly. Philip added, "She's probably in her room, plotting more evil. She spins disaster like a spider spinning a web."

Daphne said softly, "I'm sorry for her. She is a sick and unhappy woman."

"I am, too, but I'll feel better when she's behind bars."

They moved closer to the house, peering through the gray twilight.

The older officer said under his breath, "Look!"

A figure in misty white floated across the veranda and down the wide marble steps, pausing at the bottom to stoop and rise again. A burst of red blossomed on the night air, lighting Pilar's set face and upraised arm.

Daphne whispered, "What is it?"

"A torch. Pine knot, most likely. She must have had it ready."

"I don't see why—"

In the smoky, flaring light from the improvised torch, Pilar's face was set and cold, but her eyes shone with an unholy glitter. She moved swiftly and smoothly across the lawn toward the little square of window behind which Isabel and the two servants were sheltered. Daphne shivered, watching her from the shadow of the overarching trees. The scene had the unreality of some pagan rite: the white-robed woman gliding through the gray evening air, the flaming torch held high.

Philip said hoarsely, "My God, she's going to fire the stables!"

"Her own child." The older of the deputies put a hand to his holster. Daphne said faintly, "Oh, no!"

The stable door swung open. A small lopsided figure hobbled out into the open space before the building. Pilar hesitated, holding the torch above her head. Then she broke into a run, heading directly for the old man with the blazing pine knot outstretched.

Philip groaned. "They're trapped like rats. Miguel doesn't stand a chance."

The reddish light flickered over the old man, caught a gleam of metal as he lifted the clumsy musket to his shoulder. There was a moment of absolute silence. Then the shot rang out.

Pilar screamed high and shrill, like a wounded cougar, and toppled to the ground. The torch fell from her hand and dropped down her flimsy draperies. Before the watching four knew what had happened, she was a mass of flames.

Daphne said in a low voice, "The silver bullet."

Philip did not hear. He slid to the ground and ran, not to the fallen woman whose screams had stopped, but in the direction of the stable. One of the men said, "They're all mad!"

"No." But she strained to see through the thickening dark.

Miguel tottered, righted himself, and swayed again, clutching his chest. There was a dull thud as the Civil War musket fell from his hand and struck the ground. Philip ran to catch the old man as he slumped to his knees.

"Dead," he said simply as the other three gathered around. He laid Miguel's body gently back on the grass and pulled the shirt away from his chest, then bent to listen for a heart that no longer beat. The two officers slowly removed their hats, and the elder sketched the sign of the cross. "He was a good man," he said. "Folks around here respected him, even if he was a foreigner."

"He was a very old man," Philip said, "and his heart was weak. I think he'd have chosen to go this way."

"He never committed a violent act in his life," Daphne's eyes were wet. "Only to save someone he loved, he said—"

"Well, he did that. Greater love hath no man,"

Philip said reverently. "He'll lie next to my step-father in the family vault. It's what both of them would have wanted."

Daphne said, "He saved Isabel."

The stable door swung open. Isabel and Suzanne walked toward them hand-in-hand; Isabel's face was white. As she saw the fallen Miguel, she let go of Suzanne's hand, and, with a cry, ran to throw her arms around Philip. "You're my Tio Felipe really, aren't you? Miguel told me. My father is dead and now my mother and Miguel are dead, too. Am I an orphan?"

Philip cleared his throat. "Not really, *chiquita.* The court will let you be my little girl and live with me, and if Daphne will marry me, than you'll belong to her too."

"Will we live at Fairlawn?"

"That depends on my wife."

Daphne looked around. The merciful darkness was settling down now, masking the hideous scene. A cool breeze had risen. A bird chirped in the tree above her head.

The sun will shine again, she told herself, *and new grass will grow over the places where the dead lay—an unhappy woman who brought tragedy to everyone that crossed her path, and a brave and good man who gave his life to protect the child he loved. If her spirit finds peace, his has no need of forgiveness. His memory will be an everlasting blessing.*

She said slowly, "This house was built by a man for the woman he loved. If we try, perhaps we can undo the harm that has been done here."

She put one hand on Philip's arm, the other

on Isabel's shoulder. They stood in the first rays of the rising moon, linked by love.

"We'll live at Fairlawn," she said, "and we'll open all the windows and let the sunshine in."

"Amen," said Philip. He took them both in his arms.